THE READING BUDDY

BRYCE GIBSON

Cover design by Humblenations.com

The Reading Buddy/Bryce Gibson – 1st edition
ISBN: 154866118X
ISBN-13: 978-1548661182

CHAPTER ONE

A SET OF keys jangled in my hand. The keys were my lifeline. One of them would be what saved the day. I held onto them as tightly as I could.

I was being followed. The man running behind me was my stepdad, Morris Heyward. He was holding an axe.

I didn't want to look over my shoulder to see how close he was getting, and I didn't have to. I could hear him. Since the yard had not been mowed in weeks, the weeds were high and made a swishing sound against his jeans.

I wish it would have been as easy as calling for help, but my phone was useless; the screen was shattered. Minutes earlier, Morris had yanked the phone from my hand and crushed it with his steel-toed boot.

I followed a foot path into a slim set of trees and could already see the street lights on the other side. Soon after I emerged from the tree cover, the tall, uncut grass gave way to scattered gravel around the edge of the train tracks. My bare feet stumbled over the iron rails. I nearly tripped but managed to catch myself before I fell flat on my ass.

There were no cars on the road. It was nearly midnight. Nobody drove through the small town of Ridge Spring, South Carolina at that time of the night.

To my left was a line of businesses. The buildings had been built in the 1800's when the town was founded. My destination was straight ahead.

Heyward Pool and Supply was located in what had once been a gas station. The streetlights reflected from the windows that stretched across the front of the brick building.

I grasped the keys tighter in the palm of my hand. I was almost there.

I had picked up the keys by accident. In a panic to get out of the house, I'd grabbed the wrong set, but after trying to unlock my truck door, I realized my mistake. And so I had made the decision on the spot—I would go to the store.

The smooth, black asphalt of the parking lot was a relief underneath my bare feet. As I got closer to the front of the building, I could see my reflection in the glass. I was shirtless and wore a pair of jeans. My chest was smeared with drying blood. I caught a glimpse of movement behind me. I knew that what I was seeing was Morris.

After turning the key, I pushed the door open, slipped inside, flipped the lock, and spun around to face what was behind me. There was no sign of Morris anywhere. I stumbled through the dark store. I knew that there was not a phone on the property. For years Morris had been using his cell as his business line.

Everything smelled like chlorine and plastic. Giant, inflated pool toys—a whale, alligator, and an inner tube—hung from the ceiling tiles over the main aisle.

I helped at the store after school and on the weekends so I knew my way around. I made my way into the stockroom and crouched down between the desk and the bathroom wall.

This gave me a moment for things to begin to settle in my brain. For the first time, the sickening realization of everything settled over me.

My best friend—Davey Steep—was dead.

He had been killed with an axe. The same axe that Morris held in his hands now.

Davey's blood was smeared across my chest. The thought nearly caused me to puke, but instead, I started to cry.

I reached to the top of the desk and fumbled around until I found what felt like a thin rag. I grabbed onto the piece of fabric, yanked it down, and knocked over a cup of pens and pencils in the process. I realized that what I was holding was a company t-shirt. As I tried to clean the blood from my chest, the cotton fabric only smeared the half-dry blood and pulled at the hairs on my body.

Then I heard the loud shattering of glass from the sales floor. Without seeing the action first hand, I knew what had happened—Morris had made his way into the store.

I jumped to my feet and bolted across the narrow stockroom, pushing through the back door in a matter of seconds.

I made my way around the building to where a display model of the store's bestselling in-ground pool was standing on a trailer that had been parked on a thin strip of grass next to the highway. The nice, curvy shaped pool—The Big Dipper—was strapped to the trailer so that it stood upright, making the inside visible to passing cars.

From out of nowhere, a weight crashed into me, knocking me sideways. I landed with a thud against the inside of the pool display.

I tried to stand up and fight my way past Morris, but his free hand was reaching and grasping at me. He shoved me back again. When I landed against the pool, I felt the entire thing shake. I grabbed onto the edge and pulled myself forward only to meet Morris's attack again.

I felt the shift of the pool against its restraints. My butt slid across the smooth fiberglass as the whole thing began to fall forward.

Everything else happened so quickly that I didn't have time to think. There was a brief moment when Morris wasn't fighting me. Instead, there was a deer-in-the-headlights look on his face, and he was frozen in place. When he looked up, a dark shadow swept over him.

The pool had come loose from its strapping and was falling on top of us. There was only a split second of my understanding this fact before instinctively shielding my head with my hands and falling to the ground. The pool landed with a loud crack and covered the two of us in darkness.

A TOWN UTILITY worker found me at daybreak.

From underneath the pool, I heard a man's frantic voice as he made a phone call. Then, just a few minutes later, there was the sound of vehicles and slamming doors.

"Move as far back as you can," a woman yelled out to me. "We're coming in with a forklift right about here." Through a narrow gap that was between the pool and the ground, a flashlight beam danced around the grass. I scooted as far away from the light as I could and watched as two enormous metal prongs were pushed toward me.

When the overturned pool was finally lifted off of me, I saw that a small crowd had gathered around the scene. I heard shocked gasps from several of the onlookers.

I was placed onto a stretcher that several EMTs immediately began to roll away. I looked toward my stepdad's broken body that lay on the ground in the same spot where the pool had fallen on top of him. I tore my eyes away from what I was seeing, and when I flopped my head to the other side, I was met with the faces of the crowd.

Mixed in with the expressions of concern and sorrow, there was something else that I saw on the faces of the spectators. It was judgment.

From there I was sent to a mental hospital where I was kept under close watch, and a woman from Social Services was assigned to work my case.

After two months in the hospital, Social Services placed me to live with my father until I turn eighteen and free to live on my own.

My parents got divorced when I was five. Mom remarried when I was seven and then died in a car crash five years later. After Mom died, Morris had been given custody over me.

I don't remember much from the years when Dad, Mom, and I had all lived together. There are only small, brief images that come to mind when I think about that span of time—a white picket fence, a small baby goat, and the green tops of carrots growing in a garden.

CHAPTER TWO

"BLAKE, IT'S TIME to go."

It was my father yelling from downstairs.

I was sitting on the edge of the unmade bed, tying the laces on my boots. "I'm coming," I yelled toward the bedroom's closed door. "Just give me a minute."

"You've already had thirty minutes, Blake. We're going to be late."

I looked at the clock on my nightstand. He was right. The appointment with my therapist was in less than ten minutes.

I stood from the bed, ran my fingers through my hair, and grabbed my favorite cap.

"I'll be in the car." Dad yelled up to me.

I heard the sound of the front door slamming shut. The impact rattled the old windowpanes on the wall.

I knew that Dad was pissed.

As I made my way down the creaky staircase, I heard something else. It was Wolf, my dad's black Labrador. She was slapping her tail against the inside of her metal crate.

Standing at the bottom of the steps, I peeked into the den. Wolf looked at me from behind the crate's door, tilted her head to the side, and made a pathetic whimper.

From outside, there was the sound of Dad's horn.

I rolled my eyes. "I'm coming," I mumbled under my breath.

When I opened the door, Dad's truck was already running, and he had put it into reverse. The red brake lights illuminated the gravel driveway.

After shutting the front door to the house, I hustled down the driveway and opened the truck's passenger side door. "I overslept," I told him. "It's not that big a deal." By then I was sitting down. I buckled my seatbelt and slammed the truck door.

"It *is* a big deal, Blake. You're my responsibility now whether you like it or not."

The truck's tires crunched over the gravel as Dad spun out of the driveway.

Up until the past few years, Dad had lived in Georgia. I visited his home in Edgefield often, and I had already been living there for two weeks, but I still studied the outside of the house like I was a visitor.

The 1800s-era farmhouse was covered in white clapboard. There was a tin roof that was rusted in several spots. A wide front porch stretched across the front. The roof on the right side of the porch was sagging and being supported by a thick balustrade that was pressed into the ground.

Not long after backing out into the road, the truck barely paused at the stop sign at the end of the road before Dad turned the wheel to the left and drove toward town.

It was only three miles to the town limit sign, but sometimes riding with him made it fell like an eternity.

"After I drop you off, I'm going to the store," he said. "Destiny is supposed to be at the house around six. Supper is at six-thirty."

Destiny was Dad's fiancé. I had only been around her a few times. She seemed okay.

"I'm thinking spaghetti," Dad continued. "How does that sound?"

I shrugged my shoulders. "It's fine with me."

"Blake, Destiny has been looking forward to this all week. Please, just try to show a little bit of enthusiasm."

I had always been shy, but recently it had gotten a lot worse. On the first visit with my psychiatrist, she told me that I was showing all of the signs of PTSD—Post Traumatic Stress Disorder, and that the social anxiety was probably stemming from that.

I thought about the pamphlets that I had flipped through in the waiting room. According to what I had read, and what Mrs. Reynolds had told me about my "journey to recovery," there are stages to combating anxiety.

People in stage two have admitted to themselves that they have a problem.

I was in stage two.

Just a week earlier, I had been folding towels in the laundry room when I knocked over a bottle of bleach. The plastic bottle hit the floor, the top popped off, and the harsh smelling liquid poured out onto the hardwood floor. It smelled like chlorine. Like the pool supply store. Dad found me an hour later crouched down, trembling, between the washing machine and dryer.

The passing landscape of fields and orchards eventually gave way to sidewalks and prestigious antebellum homes.

Even though the two towns were less than twenty miles apart, the town of Edgefield was a stark contrast to Ridge Spring, where I had lived before. Ridge Spring was a single strip of stores, businesses, grain silos, and a train track that ran perpendicular to all of them. The center of Edgefield was a quaint, grassy square that had a gazebo at its heart and a looming brick courthouse that overlooked everything else. Because of Edgefield's violent past, legend had it that every inch of the square has been stained by blood.

"Here we are," Dad said as he brought the truck to a grinding stop in a space on the far, back corner. "I'll be back to pick you up in exactly one hour."

I got out of the truck, shut the door, and watched Dad drive away.

Mrs. Reynolds, the therapist, worked from home. The house was an old Victorian that was just off the square next to a pottery studio and museum. I walked down the crushed brick walkway to the back of the house where her office was located.

Inside, several posters had been tacked to the walls. One of the posters read PTSD—POST TRAUMATIC STRESS DISORDER—HOW TO KNOW IF YOU HAVE IT. There was a window that looked out onto a neatly mowed yard and a bookcase that was so loaded down with books that the thin, wooden shelves sagged in the middle. A potted flower sat atop a metal filing cabinet in the corner. Other than the flower, the room seemed to be devoid of any kind of personal touches.

"How have you been since our last meeting?" Mrs. Reynolds was sitting behind her large, metal desk. A manila envelope was on the desk in front of her.

I sat across from her and told her about the incident with the bleach.

The therapist didn't respond right away. Instead, she leaned back in her chair and looked me in the eyes. "Blake, I think that reading is something that you need to get back to doing. Is it a trigger? Is that the reason that you have pushed it to the side? It's normal for people in your situation to lose interest in their hobbies, but..."

"It's not a trigger. I just don't want to do it anymore."

It seemed like Mrs. Reynolds thought that everything had the potential to be a trigger that could bring back memories of that night.

"Just let me pass this along to you." She opened the folder that was sitting on her desk. "I've compiled a list of people that you can friend on social media. This is a reading buddy program..."

"Really? A reading buddy? I'm not ten years old."

Up until then, my only knowledge of reading buddies was from elementary school when the teacher had paired each student with a high school mentor. Mine had been a senior named Bethany Crane. Bethany wore the shortest shorts that I had ever seen and was always sucking on a breath mint. She was my first crush.

Mrs. Reynolds slid a pamphlet across the top of the desk.

"They will know nothing about you personally. This is just a way for you to baby-step into *somewhat* of a social relationship, and, at the same time, you'll be picking back up an old hobby. It will be preparing you to take action."

It felt weird to only be seventeen and have someone refer to something you used to do as being *old*.

And by "take action", I knew what she meant—make a friend.

I picked up the pamphlet and slid it into my back pocket without looking at it.

Mrs. Reynolds continued talking. "You are at such a crucial time in your life. It is imperative that you overcome this. You mentioned at our last meeting that you wanted to know *why* your stepdad did those horrible things."

"Well, wouldn't you?"

She nodded her head. "I'm not saying that you're wrong for looking for that sort of closure. I understand that need. I really do. But the truth of the matter is that you may never fully understand." She reached to the open folder and picked up another sheet of paper. "Here. Let me give you this."

I took the paper from her and turned it so that I could see the front. A single line ran diagonally from the bottom left to the top right where she had clipped a narrow strip of star-shaped stickers. Six circles were evenly spaced along the line and labeled with the steps to beating social anxiety—PRE-CONTEMPLATION, CONTEMPLATION, PREPARATION, ACTION, MAINTENANCE, and TERMINATION.

"It's a progress chart," she said. "Take it with you and mark your achievements."

While I was sitting in her office, I peeled two of the stickers from the paper and stuck one on each of the first two steps. The idea seemed silly, but it made me feel good. Like I was accomplishing something. Two steps down. Four to go.

AFTER THE SESSION was up, I went outside to where Dad was in the truck waiting on me.

I opened the passenger side door and flopped myself onto the seat.

He was smiling. "Hey there big guy, how did it go?"

Dad was one of the most flippant people that I knew. On the way to town he had been on my case about being late and now, just an hour later, he was calling me *big guy*? And smiling?

I pulled the reading buddy program from my back pocket, handed it to him, then pulled the door closed.

He flipped the pamphlet open and looked it over. "It looks like it might be something good for you."

He passed the pamphlet back to me and started the truck.

"I need to run by the brewery real quick," he said. "Riley's got the flyers ready."

Dad owned a small brewery that was located on the opposite side of the square. After driving over, Dad got out of the truck and met Riley on the sidewalk. Riley worked at the brewery. He was a few years older than me. He had black hair that came down to his shoulders. Riley handed Dad a thick stack of flyers that advertised the upcoming event, a night on the square complete with bluegrass music and tours of the farm.

Later that night, the entire house was filled with the delicious smelling aroma of garlic, olive oil, and tomatoes as Dad prepared dinner.

Before I moved in, Dad never turned on the fancy chandelier that hung over the dining room table. The lighting fixture had been there since the house had been built. Dad had always said that the old wires were a fire hazard.

Rewiring the old electric was something that he had been meaning to do for months, but his work never seemed to allow him to have enough time to get it done.

Dad worked two jobs. In addition to the brewery, he also worked at the factory in town. His dream was that he would one day be able to quit the factory job and focus on what he really loved doing—making beer.

Just the previous week, I'd offered to do it for him. I went into the attic where I pulled the old wires through the ceiling and replaced them with new ones just how Morris had taught me.

Destiny arrived right on time, and the three of us sat at the dining room table together, underneath the lit chandelier, and ate dinner.

"Work was crazy from the minute I got there," Destiny told us as she twirled spaghetti noodles around her fork and used her free hand to brush the long bangs out of her eyes. "I was already booked, but the walk-ins just kept coming. Everybody decided they needed to get their hair done at the same time."

Dad and Destiny continued to talk about work, and I sat in awkward silence at the end of the table. I wouldn't have had much to offer in the conversation even if I'd wanted to participate. Besides the pool store, I'd only had one other job. It was at a fast food place called Burger Heaven, and I hadn't worked there since Davey was killed.

After dinner, while Dad cleaned the kitchen, I was upstairs pacing the floor of my room.

CHAPTER THREE

THE READING BUDDY site looked legit. It was a simple black background that had the logo front and center. A horizontal row of navigation links ran across the top of the page. I clicked on the LOGIN/SIGNUP button.

Like Mrs. Reynolds had said, no personal information was required to join. All I had to do was create a username and password. I tossed a few options around in my head and finally decided on ANXIETY BOY.

After filling in my preferred genres, a list of potential "buddies" came up.

I thought that I would be able to recognize some of the ones that Mrs. Reynolds had recommended, but as I scrolled through, I realized that there seemed to be hundreds of them. I would need to do a search for the specific ones.

The pair of jeans that I had been wearing earlier that day were lying in a rumpled heap next to my bed. The pamphlet was still in the back pocket. I jumped up from where I was sitting at the desk and grabbed the paper.

Using the handwritten suggestions, I clicked on several of the buddy profiles until I found one that seemed to be the best match for me. His name was CHARLEY17.

The profiles were nothing more than a list of favorite authors, books, and genres. There an optional ABOUT field and a place for you to put a profile picture that could, of course, be anything that you wanted.

Charley17's profile picture was what appeared to be a stock image of a stack of books. According to the profile, Charley17 was an INTROVERTED BOOK LOVER LOOKING FOR A FRIEND.

After a brief moment of hesitation, I sent a buddy request.

I opened up a new browser window, and before the page was fully loaded, I heard an alert come through the speaker on my computer.

I clicked back to the Reading Buddy site and saw that I had a new message. With a click of the mouse, I opened the message folder.

CHARLEY17 ACCEPTED YOUR BUDDY REQUEST.

I reminded myself that the purpose of joining The Reading Buddy site was to fulfill the third step toward obtaining my goal. Reading books with Charley17 was preparation for making a real friend. With my progress chart in hand, I surveyed my room. I loved werewolf movies, and the walls were nearly covered with lycan related posters. There was an empty spot on the wall next to my desk so that is where I tacked the chart. Finally, I put a sticker next to step three. I was halfway there.

THE FINAL WEEK of summer vacation flew by, and, during that time, I would often wander alone through the land around the house.

I made my way down the dusty roads that cut through the fields. Some of the roads were nothing more that two tire tracks that led through the grass.

For the twelve years that I had lived in Ridge Spring, I had been surrounded by wide hay fields and crowded cow pastures. Now, the hops and scuppernongs that surrounded my new home were a welcomed change from what I was used to.

From where I stood in the field, instead of being surrounded by the color of dry straw, I saw healthy green vines that were growing along wire trellises.

Dad's land neighbored that of an old farmer named Mr. Callaway.

As I walked by Mr. Callaway's scuppernongs, I stopped briefly to peer down one of the long rows. I imagined being stuck in the field at night and not being able to find my way out.

I reached out my hand to a large cluster of the bronze-colored grapes and pulled one of them off the bunch. Even with all the times that I'd stayed at Dad's house, I had never tasted a scuppernong. I popped the entire thing in my mouth. The skin was tough. The inside was slimy and full of seeds. It was horrible, and I spit the whole thing out.

I turned back toward Dad's land and made my way down one of the rows of hops.

Apposed to the way that the scuppernongs grew on horizontal wires, the hop vines grew skyward. Like the scuppernongs, the hop vines were supported on wires, but these were attached to cedar poles that were at least twice my height.

The vines were covered in green leaves and little pinecone-looking things—the hops. No, I didn't taste one of them. I knew that they were not for eating. They were grown for adding to the various beers that Dad made in his brewery.

Finally, I found my way to a clearing that butted up to the corner of Mr. Callaway's scuppernong field, Dad's hop yard, and a dense set of woods. A pile of board and tin lay in the middle of the grass. It was the remnants of an old building. A large tree stood in the center of the land next to the pile of rubble. I made my way over to the tree and flopped down onto the ground next to a large, exposed root.

I pulled my phone out of my back pocket and opened the Reading Buddy app. In addition to the current e-book that Charley17 and I had downloaded from the site's extensive library, the app had a list of our reading history, a message folder, and a status symbol that would indicate if your reading buddy was online or not. Green meant yes and red meant no.

With my finger, I tapped the cover image of the book that we were currently reading. The book opened to the page that I had bookmarked.

The app was designed so that I could see Charley17's progress being made in yellow highlights, while he could see mine in blue. He was just a few pages ahead of me.

If one of us wanted to comment on a particular passage, all we had to do was highlight the words by tapping the screen and dragging. Then a message box would pop up. Inside this box was where comments could be typed and sent to each other. It was just like texting.

Even though I had been hesitant about the Reading Buddy program at first, it hadn't taken long for me to start enjoying it. When I was reading books with Charley17, in a weird kind of way, I felt like it was the spirit of Davey that I was communicating with through the vast space of pixels and code. And I knew that, as long as I didn't know the real identity of Charley17, I could hold on to this fantasy that I had created.

I barely got through ten pages of the book before my concentration was broken by the approaching rumble of a diesel pickup. I looked over my shoulder. I didn't see a truck, but I did see a girl that was standing at the end of one of the rows of scuppernongs. The girl appeared to be about my age. She was wearing a pair of denim coveralls. Her brown hair had been braided into two long pigtails. She was wearing a purple fanny pack around her hips. She was looking straight at me.

I noticed that she held a bunch of scuppernongs in her right hand. She put one of the grapes into her mouth and spit it out a moment later. After she did the same thing again, I realized what she was doing. She was only spitting out the hull and seeds.

Just the day before, Mrs. Reynolds told me that, in order to work toward the ultimate goal of overcoming my anxiety, I should start trying to make small talk with people. "Put yourself in social situations. Interact with others. The more you avoid it, the worse it will become," she'd said.

Now, I was in the perfect situation to practice. There was no one watching. If I embarrassed myself, it would only be to one person instead of a group. But as much as I wanted to speak to the girl, I couldn't make myself do it. It was like another person was inside of me trying to get out.

The pickup emerged from the farthest row of scuppernongs and stopped. I couldn't see the driver because of the glare of the sun on the windshield. The girl turned around, went to the truck, and climbed into the back. The truck and the girl disappeared through the trees. I had missed my chance. All the way home I felt the weight of self disappointment grow heavier with every step that I took.

Inside the house, the table was set with two plates and two glasses of water. I sat at one end of the table, and Dad sat at the other. When Destiny wasn't there, it was how we always ate dinner. I had a feeling that, before I moved in, my end of the table had been used as a place for Dad to throw his mail.

"So I guess this is it," Dad held his arms out to each side, "your last supper."

"What?" The comment had taken me by surprise. Then I realized the punch line to the awful joke—the next day I was starting school.

He laughed. "Tomorrow is a big day for you."

Just the previous day, Mrs. Reynolds had said that she was impressed with the progress that I had made over the summer. She was confident that I was ready to "take action". I was ready to make friends.

That night, after I'd gone to my room, I opened the Reading Buddy app and realized that I had a new message.

DO YOU LIKE HER?

The question caused my heart to jump. For some reason, all I could think about was the girl in the field. Then I realized that Charley17 wasn't talking about her. He was referring to a character in the book.

Charley17 was nearly a hundred pages ahead of me. I thought about trying to catch up, but I knew that I should try to get some sleep. I logged off the site, left the question hanging, and turned over onto my side facing the wall.

Sleep didn't come to me easy that night. Instead, the image of the girl in the field kept me up.

Tomorrow would be a new day, I told myself. I would start fresh. Lying in bed with the nearly full moon shining through the curtains, I told myself this—it was time to take action. When I went to school the next day, I would make a friend.

Even if it killed me.

CHAPTER FOUR

I AM A blank slate.

That is what I kept trying to tell myself on the way to school.

I was in the passenger seat, and Dad was driving.

But really I wasn't. A blank slate, I mean. The truth of the matter was that most of my new classmates had probably already searched my name on the internet. I was the new kid. They would have wanted to know everything that they could about me. My best friend's murder and the death of my step-dad had been all over the news.

The idea of strangers looking into my past made me even more anxious than I already had been. I tried to push all of those thoughts aside and focus on the here and now.

I understood that there was no sense in trying to hide what happened. I was just another kid with a messed up past. These days we're a dime a dozen. The only thing that mattered was how I presented myself.

In my mind, I could fall into one of three categories.

One—I could be cool and collected.

Two—I could use my past as a great way to gain some sympathy. Maybe even from a girl.

Or three—I could be the quiet loner who may or may not be a head case because of the things that he had witnessed.

To simplify things even further, I could either fit in or I could be ostracized.

I had one chance to prove myself. First impressions mean a lot, especially when you're seventeen.

"I'm proud of you, son." Dad spoke up from behind the steering wheel. "There's something about you that seems different today. It's like you're... normal."

I turned my head to look at him. "What is that supposed to mean?" I pinched my eyebrows in confusion.

"I just mean you seem relaxed. It's like you're not even nervous."

"I'm not," I told him and shrugged my shoulders.

But really I was wearing a mask of confidence. Inside, I was a tightly wound ball of nerves.

And I wasn't comfortable with the way I looked. I hadn't had my hair cut since the spring, and it hung down over my ears in a shaggy, unkempt appearance. Recently, the acne on my face had gotten a hundred times worse.

Mrs. Reynolds said that people with social anxiety are afraid of others seeing their insecurities. I guess she's right. She also told me that I should try not to worry about what other people thought of me. Instead, I should concentrate on genuinely getting to know them. Over the past few days I had been so nervous about starting school that I had gotten nausea-inducing headaches.

The truck had already made it all the way through town. Now, we were surrounded by freshly plowed fields. A barbed wire fence ran along the roadside.

"Blake, don't get me wrong. It's great that your being so positive and all, but..."

"Dad," I stopped him. "If you don't shut up I'm not going."

"Okay. Okay." He relented and let go of the steering wheel. He held both of his hands up in mock surrender.

The truck swerved and crossed over the yellow line in the middle of the road. There was a log truck coming our way.

"Dad," I yelled.

His hands went back to the wheel, and he regained control of the truck, jerking it back into the right lane. He laughed, and the log truck barreled past us. The driver pressed down on the horn and flipped us off. "I'm just messing with you," Dad said. "That wasn't even close."

"Why do you keep making jokes? It's like you're not even worried about me."

"I'm just trying to treat you the way that I would want to be treated if I was in your situation," he said.

Ahead, the school finally came into view.

Edgefield County High was surrounded by pines. Between the trees and the road, the twisted, pink branches of tall poke weeds reached into the fog-shrouded morning.

Dad steered the truck into the crowded parking lot and stopped.

"Good luck, Blake," he said. "If things get to be too much, just give me a call, and I'll be here in three shakes of a Billie goat's tail."

I got out of the truck and slammed the door. Behind me, I heard the truck pull away, finally leaving me on my own.

The building that loomed in front of me was a cinderblock structure that had turned gray with age and weather. A wrought-iron fence wrapped itself around the property.

I made my way down the paved walkway that led to the front door.

Inside, a banner was stretched across the hallway announcing next week's homecoming and Spirit Week. Every day would have its own theme—Inside Out Day, Stoplight Day, Inclement Weather Day, Super Hero Day, and finally, Team Spirit Day.

I felt like all eyes were on me. And they were. It wasn't my imagination. I was fresh meat. Everybody was judging me. Everywhere I looked were faces that held knowing expressions. I pushed through the crowd and made my way toward my first period classroom.

The door was open so I went inside. The teacher was standing behind her desk with her arms crossed. Besides her, I was the only other person there. I went to the desk at the back corner and sat down.

Soon, the rest of the senior class began to trickle in. After the bell rang, the teacher, Mrs. Steinman, wanted us to introduce ourselves. The idea of speaking in front of the group caused my stomach to twist and rumble.

By the time that it was my turn, my hands were wet with sweat. I was shaking with nerves. I didn't want the sound of my voice to tremble when I talked. My eyes darted around the room. Everybody was looking at me. They were waiting. I was taking too long.

"Blake," I said with a cracking voice. "My name is Blake Thomas." I felt my face turning red.

I didn't speak to anybody for the rest of the morning.

At lunch there were empty chairs at some of the tables in the cafeteria, but I couldn't force myself to sit and talk with strangers.

Instead, I went outside to a gravel area that was behind the building. A pair of vacant picnic tables were standing side by side. I sat down at the one on the left and noticed that someone had scratched some type of diagram in the wood. To me, it just looked like a jumbled mess of letters and marks.

With the day already half over, I had so far failed in my intentions of making a friend. I could only imagine what everybody thought about me and what they were saying. I knew that, if I didn't do something soon, I would likely be facing an entire year of torment and ridicule.

I was opening my paper lunch bag when I heard someone call my name. I turned around to look, but nobody was there. I pulled my sandwich out of the bag, and, just as I was about to bite into it, I heard it again.

This time, when I turned to look, I saw a thin trail of cigarette smoke coming from around the corner of the building. Then a face appeared. I recognized the guy from English class. He was wearing a ratty, black t-shirt, jeans, and a cap.

He dropped the cigarette butt to the walkway, crushed it underneath his work boot, and began walking toward me.

"Mind if I sit here?" He asked me.

I shook my head.

He straddled the bench so that he was facing me.

"My name's Cade," he said. "It's your dad that owns the brewery?"

"Yes," I told him.

He smiled and didn't say anything in return. Instead, he bent over and picked up a small rock.

I changed the subject. "Do you always come out here by yourself?"

"Me and my friend, Tristan, used to eat lunch out here everyday, but he graduated last year. He's going to Tech now. Looks like it might be just me and you this year."

"Yeah," I said. "Looks like it."

Cade threw the rock and it skipped across the pavement of the sidewalk like it would have done on a pond.

For the rest of the week I had somebody to eat lunch with. We didn't talk much, but I liked the company.

"What are you doing tonight?" Cade asked me on Friday.

"Nothing." I shrugged my shoulders.

"Well, if you want to hang out..."

Then I had an idea. "I can get the key to the brewery. Just bring your own cups."

IT WAS ALMOST midnight, and I was standing in my room, facing the wall where the progress chart was hanging. I put a star next to step four.

A moment later, I stepped out of my room and looked toward the closed door at the end of the hall. It was Dad's bedroom. Over the sound of the late-night news, I could hear him snoring.

I was careful to not make much noise as I made my way downstairs. I was holding both of my boots in my right hand.

Wolf was following me. Her nails clicked on the hardwood of the steps.

When we got to the front door, I reached into the front pocket of my jeans and pulled out five doggie treats. I knew that once the dog realized that I was leaving she would start to cry. It was a sound that would surely wake Dad. There was only one thing that would keep her quiet. Treats.

I let her take one of the morsels from my hand, and I tossed the others onto the floor.

While Wolf was preoccupied with collecting the scattered pieces of kibble, I slipped out the front door. The night air was muggy. I ran to the end of the driveway where I stopped to put on my boots.

Cade's pickup truck was parked at the end of the road. As soon as I had both of my boots on, I started to make my way there. I noticed several hunting related decals on the back glass. I swung open the passenger side door.

"I thought you decided to bail on me." Cade said and looked at his watch. "I was about to go break in there myself."

I didn't think what he said was funny, but I laughed anyway. I reached into my pocket, pulled out the key to the brewery, and handed it to him.

Cade took the key and threw it into the console's cup holder. He put the truck in drive, and we started toward town. "I hope you like country," he said and turned up the volume on the radio.

"It's fine," I told him. "I'll listen to whatever."

"Why is it that you don't drive?" Cade asked. "If you don't mind me asking."

"I have a license, but no car." I told him. Half of it was a lie. The truth was that I had a license, but I wasn't supposed to start driving again until the panic attacks began to settle down. I had a truck that was currently in Dad's backyard, covered with a blue tarp.

"So what are you into?" Cade asked. "Do you hunt?"

I shook my head. "No," I told him. "I like to read, and I like movies."

"What kind of movies do you like?"

"Werewolf ones, mostly."

Neither Cade or I talked for the rest of the drive.

"Park in the back," I told him. "That way nobody will see us."

Cade followed my instructions and guided the truck around the square. He turned down a narrow alleyway that ran behind the buildings.

We weren't alone. A vintage black truck was parked behind the brewery. I could see the shadowy image of a person inside.

"Crap, there's somebody here. Don't stop," I said.

"Calm down," Cade told me and parked next to the other truck. "That's just Tristan."

"I thought it was going to be just me and you."

Cade put the gear shift into park and turned to look at me. "Blake," he laughed and made a face like he just realized something. "You weren't expecting any kind of funny business were you? Because..."

"No." Then I realized what he was implying. "Hell no," I added. The last thing I needed was for *that* kind of rumor to get started.

Cade opened his door and got out of the truck. I sat where I was and watched him and Tristan talk. Like Cade, Tristan was wearing a ball cap, t-shirt, jeans, and boots.

I was more comfortable being with one close friend instead of a group. I didn't want to be there anymore.

Cade was unlocking the door when he turned around to look at me. He motioned for me to get out of the truck, and I did. I mean, what else was I supposed to do?

"Is there going to be an alarm?" He asked me as soon as I had my door open.

I told him that there wasn't, and he pushed the door inward. With Cade in the lead, Tristan next, and me last, the three of us entered into a small hallway that had a door on each side. The tasting room was straight ahead. "I'll get the lights," I said.

Cade and Tristan continued on down the hall while I went through the door on the right. I was standing in the brewing area, the heart of the business. Like the rest of the building, the walls of the room were made of exposed brick. Moonlight came in through two large windows on the back wall and reflected off the stainless steel tanks and brewing equipment.

The tanks were so tall that there were ladders next to each of them that the brew master would have to climb so that he could stir the mash with a long wooden paddle. The beginnings of the beer, the mash, would then be siphoned out into a fermenting tank where it would sit for several weeks. And then it would go into the kegs that were lined along the back wall. The electrical box was next to a dry-erase board that had the dates and times of the current brew. I opened the door to the box, flipped the switch, and the lights came on. Dad hated the sickly glow of fluorescent bulbs, and, just like every room at his house, all of the light fixtures in the brewery held the amber-colored glow of halogen.

When I came around the corner into the tasting room, Cade was already behind the bar. He was filling a pint glass with beer from one of the taps that ran along the back wall.

The tasting room was the most well presented area of the entire place. The bar and the walls of the small room were made of clean, polished wood.

"I thought you were bringing your own cups," I said.

"My bad. I forgot." Cade placed the full pint in front of Tristan who was sitting across from him. Cade got another glass from underneath the bar. "I'll clean them before we leave."

"Just don't break any," I said. "Riley, the guy that works here, knows exactly how many of each style they have."

"So he's OCD?" It was a girl's voice that came from behind me.

I spun around. "What?"

"OCD. Obsessive Compulsive Disorder." It was the girl from the scuppernong field. "People with OCD like to count things," she said. "They do it all the time."

I had no idea that she would be there. She must have come in when I had gone into the back to turn on the lights. She was standing in the corner where there were shelves of t-shirts and caps that all had the brewery's logo printed on them. Like before, the girl had her hair braided in two pig-tails that came down past her shoulders.

"But it's okay," she continued. "Everybody has their issues. I know I do."

Cade walked up beside me and handed the girl a full glass.

She shook her head. "Cade, you know I'd be strung up like a wild hog if my dad smelled that on me."

Since the girl turned down the beer, Cade handed the glass to me. It was the first beer that I had ever tasted, but I tried to play it cool like it was something that I did all the time.

"My name's Lisa, by the way."

"Blake," I told her.

Cade spoke up. "Lisa's homeschooled, but I figured y'all already knew each other. Her old man works for your dad and Mr. Callaway. She's going to Clemson in the fall."

"Where are you going?" Lisa was looking at me.

"I haven't decided." The plan was that I would be going to USC and be rooming with Davey who'd gotten a full scholarship. All of that was thrown out the window.

"Don't go to Tech," Tristan spoke up and downed the rest of his beer. "It sucks." I knew he was talking about Tech not the beer because he walked over to the taps and began to refill his glass. "We should party here after the homecoming dance," he said.

"You have no business at a high school dance," Lisa told him.

Tristan returned with a full glass. "Well, it just so happens that I have myself a little high school honey."

Cade patted my shoulder. "Lisa, Blake is probably looking for a date."

I felt myself turning red.

"Why don't we play cards?" Tristan changed the subject, reached into his pocket, and pulled out a full deck."

All four of us sat around one of the high-top tables. My mind wasn't really in the game. I was uncomfortable with everything that was going on around me. My eyes began to wander around the brewery, and I noticed several framed art prints that hung on the wall. There was one in particular that caught my attention—a woman wearing a period dress and holding an axe.

Her name was Becky Cotton, the Murderess of Edgefield. Legend had it that, back in the 1700s, she killed her husband with an axe. They say she haunts the area surrounding Slade Lake.

It's hard to explain, but as I recounted the legend in my mind, it was like I was seeing the murder as it took place. I could see the blood and hear the man screaming.

But it wasn't *that* death that I was visualizing. It was Davey's.

Thinking about all of that, in addition to the alcohol, made the room feel like it was spinning, and I was starting to feel dizzy. I was hot. "I'm going to step outside for some fresh air."

The night air was cool. It was pleasant. The brewery had an impressive store front that had been constructed to look like an old porch. I leaned on the rail and faced the grassy square. Overhead, the moon was bright. Other than the talk and laughter that was coming from inside the brewery, the town was quiet. I bowed my head and took several deep breaths, and when I looked up again, I saw movement out of the corner of my eye.

I stood up straight to get a better look. Something was moving around the opposite side of the gazebo. Other than the moon and the streetlights, the area was dark, and it took me a second to comprehend what I was seeing.

There was a person standing in the center of the gazebo. The figure was wearing what looked like a black rain jacket. Underneath the hood, the face was marred by dark shadow. He, or she, or *it* was staring straight at me.

I took a step back and tripped over something that was on the floor. As I fell backward, my hands reached and grabbed at the empty air in front of me. When I landed, something cut into my shoulder, and the back of my head thudded against something solid. Everything waivered in and out of consciousness.

And next, there was darkness.

CHAPTER FIVE

CADE, LISA, AND Tristan were standing over me.

"Look at all the blood." It was Lisa's voice that I heard. "There's so much. What if he needs stitches?"

I tried to sit up, but I was stopped short by the pain.

Lisa knelt down next to me. "Help me get him to his feet." She was talking to Cade. She stepped around so that she was behind me.

Following instructions, Cade moved so that he was facing me, reached out his hand, and I extended my hand to his. From behind, Lisa's hands were on each side of my waist. "On the count of three," she said. "One, two, three." Cade pulled and Lisa lifted. Then, I was standing.

Lisa let go of my waist, but I immediately wanted her hands back on my body. She lifted the back of my shirt all the way above my shoulders. I could feel the cool air on my bare skin. I heard Lisa gasp. "It's pretty bad," she said and dropped my shirt.

"I'll get my truck," Cade said and was already going back through the front door of the brewery.

"And then what?" Lisa questioned Cade's motives.

"County ER is open all night," he told her.

Lisa shook her head. "They'll need proof of insurance. We'll have to get his dad." She turned her attention from Cade toward me. "Where is your phone?"

Shit, I thought to myself. I am going to be in so much trouble. Sneaking out of the house, taking the keys, drinking... I did not want to call my dad.

I shook my head. "I can't..."

"You've got to get to the doctor," Lisa said and reached into the front pocket of my jeans. Her hand came out with the phone. She scrolled through my contacts and dialed Dad's number.

There was a long moment of silence. I knew Dad was sleeping. It was nearly two in the morning. I imagined him stumbling from the bed to get his phone. Then he answered.

"This is Lisa Tanner. Blake had an accident. I think he might need stitches. We're at the brewery." Lisa disconnected the call and slipped the phone back into my pocket. "He's on the way."

Dad was there within ten minutes. When he got out of the truck, I was relieved to see that the expression on his face was more of concern than anger.

"My God, Blake," Dad said when he saw the blood. "Get in the truck."

From the passenger seat, I watched as Dad locked the brewery and sent Cade, Lisa, and Tristan on their way.

"What happened?" Dad wanted to know after getting behind the wheel.

"I thought I saw somebody and I... I started to go back inside, but I tripped." I leaned forward. "I don't want to get blood on your seat."

I knew there were other questions that hung between us. Thankfully, none of that was brought up. But I knew that it was only a matter of time before it would be. Soon I would have to come clean about what I had done.

There was nobody else in the emergency room that night, and I was able to be seen right away. After a tetanus shot, the nurse gave me pain meds that made me feel loopy, and the doctor stitched the gash with thick black sutures.

I WOKE TO a bare room full of moonlight.

No. I realized a moment later that all of the light wasn't coming from outside. Across the room, on top of the desk, my laptop was open. I stood from the bed, went to the computer, and saw that The Reading Buddy site was up.

I placed my finger on the power button and was about to shut the computer down when I heard a thud against the hardwood floor.

The sound had come from inside the room right behind me. I stood up straight, spun around, and found myself facing someone in a black rain jacket. Because of the hood, the figure's face was covered in shadow.

My hands fumbled behind me searching for something that I could fight with, and I bumped into the computer. The whole thing fell backward and landed so that the monitor was at the perfect angle to shed light onto the intruder's face. It was my stepdad. I had seen dead fish with eyes that looked like his. I could see the purple veins that ran underneath his skin. I realized that the thud that I had heard had come from the ax that he was holding in his right hand.

He lifted the ax, swung it over his shoulder, and brought it down toward me.

I SHOT UP in the bed and found myself kicking at the sheets and blanket. Realizing it had all been a dream, my heart rate slowly began to ease back to normal. I looked around my room and it was the usual, junky space I was used to. The walls were not empty like they had been in the dream—all of my posters were there as well as the progress chart that Mrs. Reynolds had given me.

Eventually, the sound of a tractor caused me to get up. I went to the window that overlooked the hop yard and pushed the curtain aside. What I saw was breathtaking.

The tractor was making its way down one of the rows. Some sort of equipment was attached to the back that had two extended arms that seemed to be stripping the hops from the vines and dropping them in a waiting trailer.

The man on the tractor was wearing a red and black plaid button down shirt. A straw hat was on his head. I knew that the man that I was seeing must have been Mr. Tanner, Lisa's father.

My attention to the process was broken by a black double-cab truck that pulled up to the edge of the field. A man that I had never seen before got out of the truck and left the door standing open.

Once the tractor reached the end of the row, Mr. Tanner shut off the equipment and climbed down from the seat. A minute later, Dad appeared from around the corner and went over to the pair of men. After a brief exchange with the man from the truck, Dad placed his hand on the man's shoulder, but the man shoved Dad's hand away and shook his head.

I had no idea what was going on or who the man was, but it was obvious that he was upset with Dad. As the man walked back toward his truck, he stopped and looked up to where I was standing. I felt my heart skip a beat, and I dropped the curtain. A second later, I heard the front door slam shut.

By the time that I got downstairs, Dad was standing at the bottom of the staircase.

"Is something going on?" I asked.

"Cade Williston had a wreck last night."

"Is he okay? I mean, he's not hurt or..."

Dead, I wanted to add, but I left the final word hanging between us.

Dad shook his head. "He got banged up pretty bad, but he'll be fine. Riley needs some help cleaning up your mess."

OTHER THAN RILEY, the brewery was vacant.

Riley was behind the bar wiping down pint glasses with a bright yellow dishrag. I noticed that he wore wide, leather cuffs around each wrist. He placed the clean glass on the shelf and turned it so that the logo was facing the same way as the others.

"Dad said you might need my help."

"You can wipe down the tables." He tossed me a rag.

The two of us worked in silence for a few minutes before Riley spoke. "That was a really stupid thing you did."

"What do you mean?" I decided to play dumb.

"C'mon Blake, I'm twenty-one, not a hundred-and-one. I know you let Cade and those guys in here. Anybody with a brain can see that."

I hadn't been expecting to get called out on my stupid behavior. "Does Dad know?"

Riley nodded. "I'm sure he does. Rest assured that I haven't told him, but don't forget that he's not that much older than us. He's probably been around the block a few times himself. Look here." Riley leaned on the counter. It was one of the rare times that I had seen his hands become idle. "I know what you're going through."

I kept working. "You do?"

"Here, let me give you something. Riley reached both of his hands behind his neck and began to unclasp one of the three necklaces that he wore. The black leather cord dangled from the end of his fingers. "I want you to have this," he said.

I took the necklace from him and looked at the pendant that the cord was looped through. It was a silver square about the size of a stamp. It had the emblem of a tree etched into it.

"The oak tree is a symbol of truth. Somebody special gave it to me several years ago."

"Why are you giving it to me?"

"When I was your age I had a girlfriend whose parents moved away. We were only sixteen, and she had no choice but to go with them. We tried to stay together and make it work. Every Saturday we met in North Augusta at the river. Usually I got there first, but one day she tried to beat me. When I arrived, it was already too late. They were in the process of pulling the car from the water. She'd had a wreck on the bridge and drowned."

We both sat in silence for a long while.

"So what does this have to do with me or the necklace?"

"Her sister gave it to me. After the accident was a terribly dark and sad time of my life. She said that anytime I had doubts about anything, to just hold the pendant in the palm of my hand."

I put the necklace around my neck.

Riley continued. "And now, here I am, working for your dad and collecting tips so I can buy an engagement ring for somebody else."

CHAPTER SIX

I WAS WALKING along the paved road that wrapped around the opposite side of the hop yard when I heard a girl's voice come from behind me. "Hey, Blake. Wait up."

I turned to look and saw Lisa running to catch up with me. "Where are you going?" She asked me.

"I'm just walking," I told her, and it was true. I had no destination in mind.

"Mind if I join you?"

I shrugged my shoulders. "I guess not."

Now, we were walking side by side. The summer sun shone down on us with a fierce intensity. "I heard about Mr. Williston showing up at your dad's place this morning. What a jerk, right?"

I remembered the man in the black truck. "That was Cade's dad?"

Lisa nodded her head. "Yep. Mayor Williston. He's planning to open a new shopping center out on the 25 bypass."

The bypass was a new road that would divert most traffic away from the main part of town. Without people driving through, the little businesses, like Dad's, would suffer, and the franchises, like what Mayor Williston was involved in, would thrive.

"Dad did seem pretty upset," I said.

"Believe me, Mr. Williston won't stop until he gets his way. What do you say we fight back? I'm good at digging up dirt."

"Why do you care?"

"What if I told you I had my own reasons? You tell me why you stay cooped up in your room all by yourself, and I'll tell you why I have a vendetta against Cade."

I realized that what Lisa was suggesting was sort of a version of *I'll show you yours if you show me mine.* This, however, was not going to be nearly as titillating as it sounded.

I knew that, if I opened up to her and told her everything, there would be no going back. "Okay," I said. "My stepdad murdered my best friend back in the beginning of the summer. My therapist says that, because of what happened, I have an anxiety disorder. It is really hard and actually pretty impossible for me to open up to people and make friends. So, I would rather spend my time alone. You didn't already know?"

"I've heard a little bit about it. So why are you on your phone all the time? If you're so alone, who is it that you're talking to?"

"Charley. He and I read books together online."

"Kind of like a reading buddy? I had one of those when I was five."

"Okay, what's your deal with Cade?"

"He's telling people that he and I messed around."

There was movement up ahead of us. I realized that it was a buzzard that was feeding off something on the ditch bank.

Out on rural roads, it wasn't unusual to come across dead deer, possums, or raccoons that had been hit by passing vehicles. I assumed that it was one of those wild animals that the large bird was feeding on, but, as we got closer, I realized that what I was seeing was a black dog.

I had a sinking, sick feeling that Wolf had gotten out and it was her that had been clipped by a car and left to die on the roadside. The buzzard hopped away and into the taller, overgrown grass from where it eventually took flight.

Lisa hurried ahead of me. By the time that I caught up with her, she was standing over the carcass. What I saw below me was sickening. The buzzard had pulled at the guts and innards of the animal. "She must have had puppies recently."

I immediately caught on to what Lisa was suggesting. The teats on the dog were swollen and flabby.

Lisa was getting back to her feet. "How could somebody do something like this and just leave her out here?"

The idea that somebody could be so cruel and heartless tore at my heart.

I watched Lisa's eyes trail toward the long dirt drive in front of us. At the end of the dusty driveway, an old and gray ramshackle house stood in solitude. There was a single, ancient tree on the property.

"That was probably where she lived." Lisa started walking down the dirt driveway, and I followed closely behind her. The fields on each side of us were overgrown with grass that swayed in the breeze.

The yard surrounding the house was mostly dirt. I noticed now that there were countless large rocks around the oak tree. We walked up the steps of the shabby porch. A wooden rocking chair stood by the door. "I'm not sure what the lady's name is that lives here," Lisa told me. "She has always seemed nice enough though." Lisa knocked on the door, and the screen slapped back and forth in its frame.

Eventually, an old black woman who was wearing a cotton night gown appeared from the end of the hallway. "Can I help you?" The woman asked through the screen.

"My name's Lisa and this is Blake. We were just walking along and came across a dog..."

"Oh, heavens," the woman said. "Has she been hit?"

Lisa nodded her head. "I'm sorry..."

"She was always running out there on that dang road. Kept telling her she would get it one day or another." The woman turned around and began walking away from us. "Don't go nowhere," the woman called out as she was tuning the corner. "I've got something to give you."

Lisa and I both looked at each other with the same amount of confusion.

When the woman came back just a minute later, she had a cardboard box in her hands. The woman pushed the door open and stepped outside to join us on the porch. "That was real nice for y'all to come clean with what y'all did. It means the world..."

"No." I cut her off. "We didn't do it..."

"A lot of bad can come from not telling." She placed the cardboard box on the seat of the old wooden rocking chair.

Deciding that the woman was senile, I gave up on trying to convince her that we weren't the ones that had hit the dog.

The woman reached into the box and pulled out a tiny, wiggling puppy.

"Is that one of hers?" Lisa asked.

"The only one that made it," the woman said.

I stepped closer so that I could get a better look at the puppy. The dog was a rusty brown color. "Is it a boy or a girl?" Lisa asked.

"This here is a boy." The woman held the puppy out toward us. Her fingers were knobby. They reminded me of thick, gnarled tree roots. "I want you to have him." She was looking at me.

Before I had time to say anything, the woman shoved the puppy in my arms. When I finally had control over the dog, the woman was already standing on the other side of the screen door. "Go on now. You want to get home before dark. As far as my Molly goes, my oldest son is coming for supper. I'll have him bring her here and we'll bury her under the tree." She nodded toward the big oak. "When you get to be as old as I am you find that you've lost a lot over the years, but you learn to appreciate the things you did have."

I looked toward the old oak tree. So that was the deal with the rocks. They were grave markers.

"Like I said, get on. It'll be dark soon."

As we began to make our way down the steps. Lisa stopped and turned back toward the house. "Wait," she called out toward the now empty hallway. "What is your name?"

From the dark confines of the house, we heard the woman's voice. "Ziraili," she said. "It means God's helper."

"That's what you should name him," Lisa said later. "But I'd just call him Zee for short."

When we reached the same spot where Lisa had joined me, we stopped, and Lisa reached into her pocket and pulled out her phone. "What's your number?"

I told her, and a second later my phone chimed with an incoming text message.

"There," she said. "Now you have mine. If you change your mind and want my help, just give me a call."

WHEN I GOT home, Dad was sitting at his end of the dining room table. Stacks of papers were piled around him. The lamp in the corner was on and reflected off the polished wood of the table top.

Dad looked at me and ran his fingers through his hair. He took off his reading glasses and sat them on the table. He was holding a single sheet of paper in his hand.

"Mr. Williston is forcing us to close the brewery," Dad said.

"Why? He can't do that..."

"He insists that it is my fault that Cade got drunk and wrecked his truck. He says I'm being negligent. According to this," he waved the piece of paper, "we have to be completely closed and out of there by the end of the month."

I felt my stomach drop. It was all my fault. If I hadn't snuck off with the keys that night, none of this would have happened. I knew that Dad loved the brewery, and the idea of it being taken away from him because of something I did made me feel sick. Aside from all of that, what Mayor Williston was doing seemed ridiculous. Now, Lisa's suggestion of me helping her dig up something on the Willistons didn't seem like such a bad idea.

"Dad," I said. "I'm sorry about everything. It was my idea to let them in there."

"I knew it was," Dad said. "What's the deal with the dog?"

"An old lady named Ziraili gave him to me. I guess this is a bad time to ask if I can keep him."

"Take him upstairs. We'll talk about it later."

I wasn't sure if he was referring to the dog or to what I had done.

After shutting the door to my room so Zee could roam freely, I took a quick look at the progress chart on the wall. I realized that it was stupid to have rushed into trying to be friends with Cade, and now I was facing the consequences. In that moment, the last star that I'd placed represented him, his father, and all of the crap they were doing. I pulled my arm back and punched the star so hard that I felt the plaster of the wall crack behind the sheet of paper.

My hand was still throbbing when I pulled my phone out of my pocket and found Lisa's number. I hesitated. What if I was making another mistake? But I wasn't, I told myself. This was different. Lisa and I would be helping each other out. I hit dial. While I waited on her to answer, I glanced at the progress chart and felt nervous with the fact that I was giving the fourth star another shot. This time, I promised myself, I would make it work.

THAT NIGHT, WITH Zee sleeping peacefully on the floor and Wolf on the foot of my bed, I wanted to read, but my mind was so preoccupied with everything else that I knew that concentrating on the story would be impossible. Instead, I was flipping through one of Dad's brewing magazines and came across an article on how, in 79 AD, a man called Pliny the Elder made a reference to hops, calling them "willow wolf." I dog-eared the page for later and sat the magazine aside.

With my phone, I logged onto The Reading Buddy site for the first time in two days. Charley17's progress on our most recent book had far surpassed mine. He had finished, and I was only at seventeen percent. In the corner, the online status for Charley17 turned green, and, just a second later, a new message appeared on the screen.

THERE YOU ARE! I'VE MISSED YOU ☹

Until then, I had barely even thought of him as a real person. He had existed in my mind as pixels and data. Admittedly, it bothered me to think of him as someone that I could hurt. I typed up a reply.

I'M SORRY. STILL FRIENDS?

The next message I got was an auto-generated one from the site.

CHARLEY17 UPDATED HIS PROFILE PICTURE.

I refreshed the page, and the new profile picture loaded on the screen. It was an image of one of those vintage Halloween masks—a werewolf. At first, I didn't know what to think. Then I remembered that on the day that I signed up for The Reading Buddy site, I'd marked werewolves as a favorite sub genre. Even so, I still found it a little strange, creepy even, but maybe what he was doing was just his awkward way of trying to connect with common interests. I sent him a thumbs up.

CHAPTER SEVEN

MY STEP DAD, Morris Heyward, seemed okay at first.

"Blake, this is Morris. You'll be seeing a lot of him from now on," Mom told me one night in the winter.

I was sitting at the Formica-topped kitchen table. Handmade paper snowflakes were taped on the wall all around me. An open shoe box was in my hands. I was using a sharp knife to cut a square in one end.

"Morris owns the pool store in town," Mom said. "You know, on Main Street."

I paused in what I was doing, left the knife sticking out of the thin cardboard, and took a moment to study him.

He was wearing his work clothes—a blue button down shirt that had a name patch on the left pocket, a pair of pants that were a darker shade of blue, work boots, and a cap with the company logo.

Morris reached out his hand to shake mine. I pulled the blade from the box, put the knife down on the table, and placed my hand in his.

"What have you got there?" He asked me, studying the empty shoe box.

"It's a school project," I told him. "When you look through the window, if you see the groundhog's shadow, there'll be six more weeks of winter."

"And if you don't?"

"Spring is almost here," I told him.

"Blake," Mom said, "Morris is a pretty good artist. Maybe he can draw you a really nice groundhog that you can use."

Morris sat down across from me. He reached out his hand and slid a blank sheet of paper across the table so that it was in front of him. Using a pencil, he drew the most perfect standing groundhog that I had ever seen.

I was busy coloring in the trees that I had already drawn on the inside walls of the box, and Morris carefully cut out the groundhog with a pair of scissors.

He left a rectangular tab at the groundhog's feet that I folded over and dabbed with a big glob of glue. I stuck the little booger to the inside bottom of the box so that he was standing upright.

"What else needs to be done?" Morris asked me.

"I just need to cut a hole in the top of the box," I told him. "Big enough for the sun to shine through."

Morris pulled out his own pocket knife and cut a square.

When it was all done, I placed the lid on the box. Mom, Morris, and me all stood around the table. Morris pulled out his keys. There was a little flashlight on the key ring. From the hole on the top, he shined the light into the box.

At just the right angle, the groundhog's shadow loomed across the background.

Change was coming.

From then on, Mom started bringing Morris around the house a lot. Even at seven years old I knew what they were doing when they sat in the swing after I had gone to bed.

From my bed that was pushed up against the window, I could hear them. I wouldn't fully understand the desperate groans that he was making until ten years later when I found myself in a similar situation, in that same swing on the concrete pad with a girl named Katie Carmichael, who I worked with at Burger Heaven.

I'm not going to lie and say that I didn't know that Morris liked to drink. Of course I knew. I even smelled it on his breath that very first day that I met him. As he leaned down to shake my hand, I could smell it coming from him.

I knew that people drank—I was seven, not dumb. Drinking was something that grownups did after they knocked off from work.

Mom and Morris were married later that summer. It wasn't a big wedding with flowers and tons of people. Instead, they did it at the courthouse. I was the only person there to witness.

Morris moved in with us, and I liked him being there.

After Mom died in the car crash, everything changed. One morning, Morris sat down with me at the table. "You're all I've got now," he said. "You are the only person I have in the entire world."

CHAPTER EIGHT

MONDAY MORNING SUCKED.

It was six-thirty, drizzling rain, and my shoulder throbbed. The twelve-hour pain meds that I took before leaving the house had yet to kick in.

I was leaning against an old fence post at the end of our road. The lopsided stop sign was cattycorner from where I was standing. It was where the school bus was supposed to pick me up. Without the added income of the brewery, Dad was going to start working overtime at the factory, and he would no longer be able to take me to school.

From the distance, I heard the sound of an approaching vehicle. I looked up expecting to see the bright yellow bus, but it was a vintage-style pickup headed my way. The truck eventually came to a stop in front of me, and the passenger side window came down. Tristan was in the driver's seat. It was the first time that I had seen him since the night at the brewery. I assumed that he was on the way to an early morning class at Tech.

"Sucks, what happened to Cade." He said it like he was expecting me to say something back. He lifted a cup from the truck's console and spit tobacco juice into it. "Everybody says it's your dad's fault since you let us in there."

I didn't respond right away. Instead I kicked at a big clump of dandelion weeds that were growing on the ground right at my feet. "Is he doing alright?" I finally relented.

"He's supposed to be back at school tomorrow." Tristan looked in the rearview mirror and spit in the cup again. "Are you taking the bus?"

I turned to look down the road. The flashing lights on top of the approaching bus cut through the fog.

"Yes," I told him.

"Well, let me get out of here then," Tristan said. "I guess I'll see you round."

He drove away and a minute later the bus pulled up to where I was standing. After the bus came to a complete standstill, the door opened for me to enter.

It was the first time that I had ever been on the inside of a school bus, and everybody was looking at me as I made my way down the aisle. One guy had his leg stuck out and refused to move it. Instead, I had to step over. Thankfully, there was a seat at the very back. I sat and held my head down, not wanting to make eye contact with anyone. There was the sound of the door being pulled closed, and then I felt the slight jerk as the bus began to move.

Once we were going at a steady pace, and I could hear the hum of asphalt under the tires, I finally looked around, taking in my surroundings.

The boy and girl in front of me had on t-shirts that were turned inside out. To my right, a boy was wearing a cheap, brown wig that was flipped so that the underside stitches were visible over his head.

It was Spirit Week. Every day had its own theme. It was Monday—Inside Out Day. I had forgotten all about it. Like I would have done it anyway. I wondered if once I got to school I would find out that I was the only one that hadn't participated, causing me to stick out like a sore thumb.

I turned my attention away from the other students and looked out the window.

As the bus passed through town, I saw that most of the businesses had decorated with the school colors of green and orange in anticipation of Friday night's game. Crepe paper streamers and balloons were everywhere.

Once we were past the courthouse, the bus jostled over the old, unlined road for several miles and eventually pulled up to the front of the school. I waited in my seat until all of the other kids got off the bus and then made my way down the steps.

The first thing that I noticed when I walked through the front doors was the wide, paper banner that had been painted with bright blue and orange letters.

HOMECOMING DANCE THIS SATURDAY!

I didn't talk to anybody all morning. At lunch, I sat outside at the same picnic table where I had sat the week before, but it seemed strange without Cade there. Somehow I managed to trudge through the rest of the afternoon. I barely paid any attention in my classes. All I could think about was going home.

LISA WAS WAITING for me on the front porch when I got off the school bus.

Like the other times that I had seen her, her hair was in two pigtails. By then I assumed that it was her usual style. She was wearing a pair of jean shorts, a white t-shirt that was tucked into the high waistband, and the purple fanny-pack was around her hips. She was holding her hand up and waving at me as I made my way down the gravel driveway.

Once I was on the porch, Lisa stepped to the side so that I could unlock the door. She followed me into the house where I immediately threw my book bag on the couch.

"So what is it like to ride the bus?" Lisa wanted to know.

"Really?" I asked sarcastically and turned to look at her.

"Sometimes I feel sheltered because I haven't experienced things like that," Lisa explained. "Remember, home schooled right here."

"Yeah, you're really missing out on all of the important things in life," I teased.

"You know what else I've never done? I've never gone to a dance."

"How about we take the bus to the dance Saturday night?"

Lisa laughed and let herself fall back against the wall. "You know, you sell yourself short, Blake Thomas. You're hilarious to be around."

It made me feel good that Lisa was laughing at my jokes so I continued. "If we take the bus, you'll be able to kill two birds with one stone. The school bus *and* the homecoming dance."

I went into the living room with Lisa trailing behind me and opened the door to Wolf's crate. The big Labrador jumped out and nearly knocked me over when she reached her paws up to my chest.

A smaller crate was next to Wolf's. Zee was inside. His short tail was flipping left and right. Wolf followed me, and I opened Zee's door. As the puppy skittered across the floor, his excitement was so obvious that his whole butt-end was swishing back and forth. Dad had decided that I could keep the puppy, and Mrs. Reynolds said that it was a good idea. She said that bonding with the dog could help reduce tension and anxiety.

"Speaking of killing..." Lisa spun the fanny-pack around so that it faced the front. She unzipped the largest pouch. "While I was digging up dirt in the library last night, I found this." She pulled a piece of paper out of the bag, unfolded it, and handed it to me.

It was an old, photocopied newspaper article. I took a minute to read it. According to the short article,

Mayor Williston, Cade's dad, was arrested for deer hunting out of season.

"So what? He was arrested for out of season night hunting. It's not that big a deal." I handed the paper back to her. "People do it all the time. And this article is almost twenty years old."

"Well, but there may be more to it," she said. "Let me show you where it happened." She grabbed my hand and pulled me toward the front door.

"Ahem!" I mocked the sound of clearing my throat as a way to grab her attention. "The dogs," I pointed out.

Both of them, Wolf and Zee, were sitting side by side. They were looking up at us with the epitome of expectant, puppy-dog eyes.

"Oh. Right." Lisa giggled and let my hand go.

I reached onto the lowest shelf of the antique table that was next to the door and pulled out two leashes, one of which I handed to Lisa. I clasped mine onto Zee's collar and Lisa followed suit but with Wolf.

"Okay," I said. "*Now* we can go."

THERE WAS A spot on the other side of the hop-yard that was so perfectly serene that it seemed like it had been ripped from the pages of a fairy tale.

To get there, we had to walk along a dirt road that was dry as bone underneath our feet. Wrens flittered in the vines all around us. We followed the path all the way through the hop-yard until we emerged on the other side.

The collapsed building was on our left, and Zee pulled on his leash in an effort to explore the rubble of weathered board and tin.

"Daddy shot a big rattlesnake out here last summer," Lisa said. She was holding her hands up, several feet apart, to emphasize the length.

The mention of the snake caused me to look closer at where I was stepping. I pulled on the leash guiding Zee away from what was arguably the snakiest place in sight.

"There's an old man down the road that says he can hear a rattlesnake from miles away. He can smell 'em too. He says they stink like a wet dog." Lisa scrunched her nose at the description she was giving.

I followed Lisa's lead through thicker weeds and bramble.

"Daddy says we shouldn't have to worry too much right now though. The snakes don't particularly like this kind of weather."

The weather had turned cooler over the past few days. It was only the beginning of September, but there was already a slight hint of fall in the air. So much so that I wished I had worn a light jacket. The cool wouldn't last though. The weatherman was predicting temps back in the nineties by the end of the week.

On the other side of the building we hung a sharp right. Then there was an abrupt, steep incline of several feet. A line of pines and oaks grew across the higher land. Lisa stepped up, following a well-worn path through the trees. I trailed behind.

A thick plume of black smoke rose up from the neighboring peach orchard where a tractor was pushing dead trees into a burn pile. A freshly plowed field stood in front of us. Mixed in with the odor of the close fire, I could smell the recently turned dirt. Without warning, the smell brought to mind images from long before.

I must have been a few years old at the time. A toddler, maybe. It was night. A full moon. I was crouched down low, peeking from behind a picket fence at a woman in a hooded red cloak. She was standing in the center of a freshly tilled garden plot.

"This is it. This is the land where Mr. Williston shot the deer that put his butt in the slammer," Lisa told me, shattering the vague pieces of recollection.

"So?"

Lisa nodded her head. "Daddy rents it from him."

It took me a second for what she was saying to sink in. If part of Mayor Williston's charge had been for trespassing, like the write-up in the paper claimed, it couldn't have been on his own land. He might have owned the land now, but he hadn't back then.

"Let me show you something." Lisa spun the fanny-pack around and unzipped the pouch. She reached in and pulled out a couple pieces of paper and handed them to me. "This is more snooping that I've been doing."

The first paper was another newspaper article dated from nineteen ninety-six. The headline read WILLISTON HUNT CLUB TO OPEN THIS SEPTEMBER. Attached to the article was a photo of a group of men wearing camo hunting gear. Three of the men were kneeling in the front while the other three were standing behind. They were all holding hunting rifles.

Lisa leaned over and placed her finger on the photo pointing at one man in particular. I pulled the paper closer to my face so that I could get a better look at the person that she was trying to show me. My heart nearly leapt out of my throat when I realized who I was looking at. In the photo, Dad could not have been much older than I was now.

Lisa reached into the fanny pack and pulled out more papers. "It appears that your dad and Mr. Williston used to be friends." She handed the paper to me. They were all photos of the Hunt Club. I saw Dad laughing with the other members. Some of the pictures were taken inside the building. The last photo was one of the exterior of the hunt club. It was a small square building made of board.

I lowered the picture and turned to look at the pile of rubble that was on the land next to us. "You think that was the clubhouse?"

"It appears so, and this last picture is the one that really got my goose." She pulled one more photocopy out of the pack. This one she held up and turned it so that the front was facing me.

OFFICIAL MEMBER OF WILLISTON HUNT CLUB. It was a certificate that had been signed and dated on the bottom right.

"Daddy was part of their little group too. Daddy, your dad, and Mr. Williston must have had some sort of falling out over the years for Mr. Williston to be pulling the junk with trying to close the brewery, and I'm going to find out what it is."

"Is it going to be that easy? I mean..."

"I'm going straight to the source. Friday night Cade will be at the football game and his dad is supposed to emcee the half-time event. The Williston house will be wide open."

I was worried about what Lisa was planning. Mayor Williston didn't seem like the type of person to take someone snooping in his business lightly.

All of a sudden, from my left, there was the yipping sound of Zee's barking. I spun to look and saw a huge black snake—a cottonmouth—slithering through the dirt, headed right for the puppy. I jerked on the leash, pulling Zee backward.

A deeper, louder bark came from my right. Wolf moved with such force that she jerked the leash from Lisa's hand.

As I was pulling Zee away from the approaching danger, Wolf ran past, kicking up dust. The Labrador pounced, and in one fluid motion, she clamped the snake in her jaws, killing it instantly.

After returning to the house, we let Wolf and Zee back inside, and I stood on the porch with Lisa. Off in the distance, dark storm clouds were coming in. There was the faraway rumble of thunder.

"Looks like I should be heading back home," Lisa said. "I don't won't to get caught in a downpour." She started down the steps.

"By the way, I was being serious about the dance," I said.

She stopped and turned to look back at me. "Really?" She smiled. "Well then, I would love to be your date."

"Yeah, me too." Then I realized the silliness of what I said.

Lisa laughed.

After she was gone, I went inside, locked the door, grabbed my book bag from where I had thrown it on the couch, and went upstairs. Wolf and Zee followed me into my room. I sat at the desk and tried to do my homework, but, no matter how hard I tried, I just couldn't concentrate. Finally, I gave up. Calculus could wait.

I opened my laptop and cruised around on the internet for a few minutes before logging on to The Reading Buddy site. Before I had a chance to look, I heard the sound of my phone ding with an incoming message. The phone was somewhere on the desk, underneath the flipped upside down textbooks, notebooks, and loose papers.

When I finally found it, there was a photo on the screen. It was a selfie from Lisa. She was wearing a white dress. I realized that what she was showing me was what she would be wearing to the dance on Saturday night. I jumped at the easy opportunity to flirt with her.

Obviously, I'm a boy, and boys really don't put much thought into what we might wear, and if we do, we wait until the last minute. I put the phone down and went over to the old pressboard dresser on the other side of the room and opened the bottom drawer. It was where I kept everything that I hardly ever wore.

I reached underneath a stack of folded t-shirts and pulled out the darkest pair of jeans that I owned. I stripped down to my boxers and pulled on the pants. I had lost a lot of weight over the summer, and the jeans were too loose on my thin frame. I had to put on a belt to keep them up. Then I pulled on a white button-down shirt and tucked it in. I dug in my sock drawer until I found a blue bow-tie that Mom had made me wear to church one Easter when I had been in elementary school.

After I was dressed, I stood in front of the mirror. With a comb, I parted my unwashed hair straight down the middle. Not too bad, I thought. I held my phone up and took a picture of my reflection. I reasoned that if I sent the picture to Lisa, it could go one of two ways—she would think my efforts were cute or she would laugh her ass off at my expense. It was a gamble I was willing to take, I hit send.

A few seconds later I got a reply.

HUBBA HUBBA! ;)

I smiled and felt myself blushing. As I was passing by the desk, I glanced over at the computer and saw that I had a new message from Charley17.

WHAT ARE YOU DOING THIS WEEKEND?

Mrs. Reynolds told me that, as I progressed, I would have to learn how to juggle many things: friendships, work, and hobbies. Lisa and Charley were already testing me on all of that.

Still standing, I hunched over the keyboard and quickly typed up a reply.

I'VE GOT PLANS. A GIRL.

I looked at the bottom right of the screen and saw the dot, dot, dot, which indicated he was typing up a reply. I imagined a pair of fingers drumming on a tabletop. And finally...

DOING WHAT?

CHAPTER NINE

COLLEGE SIGN-UP DAY was a big deal.

I trailed behind the rest of the class as we made our way like a herd of cattle along the covered breezeway that connected the main part of the school to the gym.

It was nearly three months until basketball season would start, and the inside of the gym felt empty. The goals were pulled up and both sets of bleachers were collapsed in on themselves. The building smelled like sweat and floor polish.

Fold-out card tables had been set up in a large square around half of the court floor. The representatives, all who looked like college students, were standing at their tables with pamphlets, clipboards, and brochures in hand.

A group of overly ambitious girls pushed past me to get to the table that they had their eyes on. It was hard to tell if it was the school or the rep—a tall, athletic guy—that they were most interested in.

I approached a table that didn't have a soul anywhere around it. Even the rep's chair was vacant. There was nothing on the tabletop except a thin stack of pamphlets and a clipboard where you could sign up to request additional information. I picked up the clipboard and noticed that there was only one name on the paper.

CHARLEY.

There was no last name. With my eyes, I followed the line across the paper to the email block that was on the far right side.

CHARLEY17@THEREADINGBUDDY.COM

A chill ran up and down my spine. Goosebumps covered my arms. I dropped the clipboard to the table where it clattered and fell to the floor. I turned to walk away and was stopped dead in my tracks by the harsh sounding screech of metal chair legs on the polished floor. I looked over my shoulder. Where there had been nobody just a second earlier, a man was now standing from the chair.

"Are you interested in going to school with us?"

He was older than any of the other reps. He was bald, chubby, and was wearing a generic cotton polo that had a wrinkled collar.

"I – I don't know," I told him. "I'm just checking things out right now."

"Well, it *is* a big decision. It's the rest of your life that we're talking about. We can send you more info if you wish." He came around the table, picked up the clipboard from the floor, and held it out toward me. "Charley would love to have you join him."

I SHOT UP in the bed. My heart was hammering in my chest. I reached over to the nightstand and picked up my phone. It was only six-thirty in the evening. For a second I thought I had been out all night. Realizing that I had been in the middle of another bad dream, I flung myself backward onto the bed.

Big. Ass. Mistake.

Beginning at the tender wound on my shoulder, the pain shot through the right side of my body. I needed a dose of pain meds, like, now. No, scratch that. I needed it an hour ago.

I stood from the bed and started to make my way to the bathroom when I caught my reflection in the mirror that hung on the back of my bedroom door. I was still wearing the clothes that I had fallen asleep in. Now my shirt tails were out. My bow-tie was loose and askew.

In the bathroom, I opened the medicine cabinet and took one of the pills from the orange bottle that I kept on the bottom shelf. Not a second after I popped the pill in my mouth, I heard a high-pitched, piercing howl coming from downstairs. It was a sound that made my skin crawl.

A second later, the howl turned into a deep, steady bark. It was Wolf. And right along with her was another bark, this one smaller and higher pitched. Zee.

I stepped quietly down the hall. From the top of the stairs I could see Wolf pacing at the door. Her tail was swishing back and forth. Her ears were perked. Based on the dog's frantic, quick movements, it was obvious that somebody was outside. In a frenzy, Zee was skittering and sliding about the floor all around the older dog.

I slowly made my way down the steps. My heart was hammering behind my rib cage so fierce I could feel the throbbing of my pulse all the way in my throat. Midway down the staircase I stopped. I was close enough that I could clearly see the deadbolt. It was turned to the left. Unlocked. My stomach went queasy.

Obviously I hadn't, but I was *sure* that I had locked the door when I'd come in from the walk with Lisa. And Dad wasn't supposed to get off work till eight so I knew it wasn't him that had left it that way.

I would feel better if the door was locked. That way, just in case, whoever Wolf was barking at couldn't come inside. I hurried down the rest of the steps, taking them two at a time. As soon as I was at the door, I reached my hand to the lock and flipped it to the right. Then, I pushed the curtain back just an inch. It was enough for me to see outside. Nothing was there.

The sky was dark with storm clouds. Wind gusts were causing tree limbs to sway and bend at scary angles. The rain came down in heavy repetitions pounding on the tin roof of the porch.

Had it been the storm that had caused Wolf's reaction? I had heard that it wasn't unusual for pets to act that way during inclement weather. My heart rate began to settle, and I let the curtain spring back into place.

Then there was a dull thump from somewhere inside the house. It sounded like something solid against the wood floor. I remembered the dream where my step-dad had stood in front of me and how he had let the axe slip through his hand. That was exactly what I was hearing now sounded like.

Deciding that the noise was probably just a tree limb hitting the outside of the house, I pressed on, walking toward the living room. I needed to check just to make sure. There was another thud. This one identical to the first. I was right. It wasn't on the outside wall. The sound was lower, on the floor. It was coming from inside the house.

After rounding the corner, standing at the threshold, my eyes scanned the living room. The corners were dark and full of shadow. But even in that darkness, I saw movement on the left side of the room. Someone turned on the lamp, and the corner of the room was lit in a soft, orange glow. I was frozen in place until I realized what I was seeing.

Dad was sitting in the chair. It was obvious to me now that the pair of thuds that I had heard had been the sound of him taking off his heavy work boots and letting each of them fall to the floor. He looked up at me and laughed. "What are you wearing?"

I felt myself turn red with embarrassment. I hadn't told him about the dance. "The homecoming dance is Saturday," I muttered.

"Oh," he continued. "That's right. This is Spirit Week. Today was Homecoming Preview Day. I'm glad you participated."

I stared at him, dumbfounded. I thought it was funny that he hadn't even considered the idea of me actually going to the dance, but if that's what he wanted to think, at least the explanation would be easier on my part. "Yeah," I said, not wanting to explain anything else. "I thought you wouldn't be home until later."

"They let me leave early. And besides, I'm beat." He sighed and stood from the chair. "I'm going to head upstairs for a quick shower." He was making his way across the room. "Oh, by the way, I brought that box inside. It had your name on it." He pointed toward the coffee table in front of the couch where there was a rectangular box sitting on top. I hadn't even noticed it until now.

"Is that what all the barking was about?" I asked. Wolf must have been worked up over the mail carrier stepping onto the porch.

Dad nodded his head. "Open it," he said. "Let's see what's inside.

I went over to the box and put my phone down on the floor. The movement caused the phone to wake up. Lisa's picture was still there. I looked up at Dad who was looking down at the phone.

"Is that Mr. Tanner's daughter?"

I nodded and pressed the button on the side of the phone causing Lisa's picture to disappear. I was embarrassed.

"She doesn't go to school with you," Dad stated matter-of-factly. He looked confused.

Dad reached into his pants pocket and pulled out his pocket knife. He flipped the blade out and handed it to me. The packing tape popped from the pressure of the blade's tip. I sliced the tape all the way down the length of the box. With both hands, I opened up the top flaps. Wolf and Zee were right beside me, eager to see what was inside.

There was a crumpled mess of brown packing paper that I removed and dropped to the floor. Then, from inside the box, a girl's deep blue eyes were staring back at me.

CHAPTER TEN

IT WAS THE cover of a book.

On the illustration, a blonde girl was turning away from a curtained window. She had a terrified look on her face. A dark figure stood on the other side of the glass, looking in. The title of the book was THE WATCHER. It wasn't the only book in the box. There was a stack of others that were the same size. I took several of the thin paperbacks from the box and placed them next to me on the floor.

As I worked, I noticed a familiar scent that clung to the box and its contents. It was a sweet, flowery fragrance. I recognized it right away. It was the perfume that Davey's mother liked to wear. In fact, she had been wearing it the first time I ever saw her.

After Mom's car crash, I spent a lot of time in Morris's store. I would go there every day after school. Usually I hung out in the back, but sometimes I helped stock shelves. One day, in the middle of October, I was on the floor, busy organizing a shelf, when I heard the familiar ding of the front door opening.

I peeked through the shelving unit. Along with a flurry of bright orange leaves, the bottom of a fur coat trailed behind the woman that entered. Her wavy blonde hair brushed her shoulders. She looked like a movie star. There was a boy with her. Like the woman, he had yellow-blonde hair. He was wearing a pair of baggy jeans and a plain black t-shirt.

"Ding ding!" The woman called out, mimicking the sound of the door chime.

"Mom!" The boy that was with her sounded embarrassed.

"Davey, we've got to get the attention of the clerk. Ding, ding," she said again.

I stood up and rounded the corner. "Can I help you?" I asked.

The woman held her hand out to me. I put my hand in hers. "I'm Miss Janice Steep," she said. "And this is my son, Davey. We're going to be moving here soon." She pointed across the width of the space. "Anyway, that pool out by the road. I would like to know about it."

I went and got Morris from the stockroom. He led the woman outside, leaving me and the boy, Davey, in the store. I went back to work, but every so often I would glance over at Davey who was leaning against the wall.

Now, as I looked through the stack of books, I placed them on the floor on top of one another, building a new stack. There were seven books in all. All of them had similar covers with colorful sketches of terrified teenagers and bright, neon titles.

A letter sized white envelope was tucked into one of the thin volumes closest to the bottom. I slid the envelope from the pages. My first name had been printed on the outside of the envelope in fancy, cursive handwriting. Other than my name, the envelope was blank. The envelope wasn't sealed. Instead, the flap had been tucked inside. I lifted the flap and slid the contents out. It was a single, folded piece of paper that had the same handwriting as what was on the envelope.

BLAKE,

I HOPE YOU ARE DOING BETTER. I TRULY HATE TO SEE YOU GET HURT. AS YOU KNOW, YOU ARE LIKE A SON TO ME.

PLEASE, LET'S GET TOGETHER SOMETIME SOON. I MISS YOU SO MUCH.

THE BOOKS THAT I'M SENDING YOU ARE SOME OF THE ONES THAT I HAD WHEN I WAS A TEENAGER. I WANT YOU TO HAVE THEM. I'M SURE DAVEY WOULD WANT THAT TOO.

CALL ME ANYTIME. OR WRITE. OR TEXT. YOU MEAN THE WORLD TO ME.

LOVE ALWAYS,
JANICE

I lowered the paper. It was the first time I had heard from Miss Steep since Davey's funeral. I missed her.

After our first meeting in the store, Davey started going to school in Ridge Spring, and we quickly became friends. We spent a lot of time together at his house and mine. It wasn't just him that I was close to. Miss Steep's presence had helped fill the void that Mom's death left behind. She treated me the same as her own son. On my birthday, I was shocked when Davey confessed to me that the money inside my card was the same amount that she had given him.

CHAPTER ELEVEN

IT WAS TUESDAY. Stoplight Day.

The halls of Edgefield County High were full of students that were wearing red, yellow, and green. I had already heard that there was an underlying meaning to the colors: green meant you were single, yellow signified that you were somebody's friend with benefits, and red told others to stay away because you were taken.

At lunch I went outside to where the picnic table sat empty amid the gray, gloomy day. On TV that morning, the weatherman had predicted that the last of the storm clouds would be out of the area by mid-afternoon. It would be a beautifully clear night full of shining stars and the soon-to-be full moon, he had said.

As I was sitting down, I noticed that all of the old scratches on the tabletop had been written over with black marker. It made the whole thing clear to me for the first time. At the top, someone's initials were written in capital letters: WHC. Even though I tried, my mind couldn't immediately connect the initials with anyone that I knew. Below the initials was a horizontal line that separated the rest of what was there into some kind of chart. There were three columns: C, T, and B; each was separated by a vertical line. The C column had five hash marks, the T column three, and B was empty. That wasn't all: something else looked different about the letter B. I placed the palm of my hand flat on the wood and ran it over the diagram. Everything there, except for the letter B and the fifth hash mark under C, had been cut into the wood and then traced over with the black ink; it had all been there before. But the B and the fifth mark only existed in ink. They hadn't been carved into the wood. They were new.

Finally, after giving up on trying to make any sense to what I was seeing, I dropped my book bag to the ground and sat down. I reached into my bag and pulled out my lunch. I put the paper bag on the table and ripped it all the way down the side so that it was splayed open like a placemat. The bag covered the whole confusing image that was now underneath. I unwrapped my sandwich from the tinfoil and was about to take a bite when I noticed something else: it was a glaringly white corner of paper that had been shoved into one of the cracks between the boards of the tabletop. I pinched my fingers onto the paper and pulled it free.

It was an index card that had been folded over several times into a thick, cardboard-like square. I unfolded it and saw a crudely drawn picture of a girl. Really, it was barely more than a stick figure, but the hair—two pigtails—made it unmistakable as to who the picture represented. FOR A GOOD TIME CALL LISA TANNER was written below the girl. I closed my hand around the index card and crumpled it into my fist.

I heard someone walk up behind me. I turned to look and was not surprised to see Cade. He was standing with a pair of crutches, one under each arm. His right leg was in a cast. It was the first time that I had seen him since Friday night. Even though I had missed having him with me at lunch on Monday, at that particular moment, because of what I had seen, just the sight of him made me angry. It caused red-hot rage to boil inside my body. He was wearing a yellow polo, a false claim, I thought.

"What the hell is this?" I unfolded the index card and slammed it down on top of the table, face up.

Admittedly, confrontation was something that was *way* out of character for me, and just the thought of it usually made me nervous. So, needless to say, because of my actions, I could feel my pulse thrumming in my throat.

Cade laughed. "Well, thanks for asking me how I'm feeling, Blake. My leg's broken by the way, but, other than that, I'm doing fine."

He hobbled closer to where I was sitting until he was standing right behind me. He had the audacity to grab onto my lunch bag and slide it out of the way. The chart was facing me again. "It's our club," he said and placed his hand on my shoulder. "I went ahead and wrote you in. I tried to get you your first score Friday night..."

Part of what I was seeing became clear. The letters at the top of each column...

C – Cade.

T – Tristan.

And, B – Blake.

I felt a pit forming in the bottom of my stomach. I had a sinking, sick feeling about everything that I was hearing. There was more going on than I wanted to be part of, more than what I even wanted to *know* about.

"What do the marks mean?" I didn't look up at him as I talked.

"Girls, Blake." He said it like I was stupid. Naïve. "Those marks represent girls."

So that was it. It was all a game to see who could score the most. And to make it worse, Cade was exaggerating his "achievements". He was spreading rumors that he had done things, things with Lisa, that he hadn't.

"You're crazy," I said. "I'm not going to be part of anything like that."

Not wanting to hear anymore, I began gathering up my stuff. I wadded the lunch bag, tinfoil, and sandwich into one palm-sized mushy ball. I hadn't even taken one bite of the sandwich. I stood from the table, grabbed my book bag, and pushed past Cade. I threw my uneaten lunch into the trashcan that was next to the school doors.

Before I went inside, I turned to look at Cade one more time. He had followed me. We were standing just a couple of feet apart. "Leave her alone, Cade. Leave both of us alone."

"You've got it all wrong, Blake. The thing is, after Lisa and I hooked up, I told her that it was just a one time thing, but she won't stop pestering me about it."

We stood there staring at each other. My arms hung straight down my sides. I started to clench my right hand into a fist.

"And in case you hadn't figured it out by now, that newest mark on the table," Cade said, "that one's Lisa."

I'm not an idiot like he thought. I *had* figured it out, but the thing is, it wasn't true. What he was saying was nothing but a lie.

A lot of what was going wrong in my life could be blamed on Cade and his father. Anger built up inside of me until I couldn't take any more. I let my book bag slide off my left shoulder and all the way down my arm to where it hit the ground. I clenched my right hand into a fist, pulled my arm back, and took a powerful swing at Cade's face. It was the first time that I had ever punched somebody, and admittedly, it felt great. If need be, I would do it again in a heartbeat.

Cade fell to his knees. The crutches clattered to the concrete on each side of him. His hand went to the side of his face where my fist had landed. I noticed a dark, steady stream of blood was pouring from his nose.

Mrs. Reynolds had told me once before that, when I was ready, I would need to commit myself to changing. It was only then that I would begin to achieve my goals, she'd said. Well, here you go, boss lady...by punching Cade, I had cemented myself on where I stood—Lisa was a friend that I was willing to fight for.

And Cade, an enemy.

DAD HAD TO leave work early so that he could pick me up.

From the open doorway of the principal's office, I watched Dad enter the building. I could tell that he was pissed as soon as I saw how he swung open the school door. Once inside, he immediately headed my way, taking long, meaningful strides to get there. White, dusty residue clung to the blue fabric of his work clothes.

I was holding an icepack to my swollen, black eye. Unfortunately, the fight hadn't ended with Cade's bloody nose. After swinging the first punch, I had learned right away that Cade was far more experienced at rough-housing than me. He only stayed down for a few seconds before standing up without his crutches. He balanced on one leg and slammed his fist into my face. It was like he was some kind of demented super-villain or something.

"What happened?" Dad asked.

Mr. Ruff spoke up from where he sat behind the desk. "Your son got into a fight."

"Blake, what the hell..." Dad spun his attention from Mr. Ruff so that he was facing me.

"Language, sir," Principal Ruff said.

"Sorry," Dad apologized. "Who were you fighting with?"

I didn't answer him. I knew that once he found out that it had been Cade, things would only become a thousand times worse.

"It was Cade Williston," Principal Ruff spoke for me.

I winced at the words and sunk lower in my chair.

Dad didn't say anything. He looked at me with a look that was equal amounts disappointment and anger.

"I'm suspending him for the rest of the week. That means no homecoming dance."

Needless to say, the ride home from school was terrible. Not only because of the fact that Dad was pissed at me, but there was also the added confusion that I was feeling—I felt bad for making Dad miss work.

I knew that he was worried about being able to make enough money to be able to provide for me. Now I was screwing everything up. And there was also the fact that I would hurt Lisa's feelings once she found out that I couldn't take her to the dance.

"I can't just drop everything that I'm doing to come rescue you out of this kind of bullshit, Blake. And Cade Williston of all people?"

I sat in silence for a moment before speaking.

"That's probably why mom was given custody over me instead of you." I regretted my words as soon as I said them.

Dad slammed on the brakes and swerved the truck over to the side of the road. "Listen to me..." He unbuckled his seatbelt so that he could lean closer to me. I couldn't tell if he was angry, sad, or...like me, there must have been several different emotions running through his body all at once. He was carefully contemplating his next words. "Just because she and I couldn't be together does not make me love you any less."

We sat that way, staring into each others eyes for too long. The tension was thick.

Finally, he flung his body back onto the seat. He bent his head backward so that it was leaning against the headrest. He closed his eyes.

"I am trying so hard," he told me. "Whatever it is between you and Cade Williston has got to come to a stop, you hear me?"

I wanted to ask him why Mayor Williston had such a grudge against him, but I didn't want him to know that Lisa and I had been snooping.

Once home, I immediately went to my room, and texted Lisa.

I MESSED UP. I GOT IN A FIGHT WITH CADE. SUSPENDED NOW. WON'T BE ABLE TO GO TO THE DANCE. I AM SO SORRY!

Later, Dad woke me from a nap by tapping on my bedroom door.

He eased the door open. "I made you some chicken noodle soup," he said. "I thought it might make you feel a little better."

I was laying on my side, facing the wall. I didn't respond, and after a few seconds, I heard him begin to walk away. "It'll be on the stove when you're ready," he said.

CHAPTER TWELVE

"Here's something else," Lisa said. "Take a look at this." She handed me a thin stack of papers.

Because of my being grounded, Lisa wasn't supposed to be there. Dad wouldn't be home from work until eight-thirty; what he didn't know wouldn't hurt him.

The midday sun beamed down onto where we were sitting on opposite ends of the wide porch steps. We each had a glass of tea; hers with a lemon slice on the rim. Wolf and Zee were lying in the grass in front of us. More than ever, I wanted to help Lisa get even with Cade. Now it had become personal.

I immediately recognized the papers as black and white printouts from a game camera. Hunters often mount the battery operated cameras on trees and deer stands. The cameras take pictures of anything that moves letting the hunters see what deer are coming to the field during the overnight hours.

Every time that I've ever looked at pictures from one of the cameras, I've flirted with the idea of what if I saw something *else* on one of them. Some weird, unexplainable creature lurking in the night; something like Big Foot, South Carolina's Lizard Man, the ghost of Becky Cotton, or a man in a rain jacket.

"Where did you get these?" I was flipping through the stack. There were deer on almost every picture. The camera used night-vision, and the eyes of the deer seemed to glow.

"There's a camera in the field where the hunt club was located," Lisa explained. "It's where Cade and his dad used to hunt."

She reached into her front pocket and pulled out her phone. She tapped her finger against the screen a few times and then held the phone face forward toward me. I was looking at a page from Cade's social media. "Look at his cover photo," she said.

I did. It was a green-tinted image of a deer with glowing white eyes. It was another picture from a field camera.

"Okay," I told her. I didn't see what any of this had to do with trying to find something to pin on Cade and his father.

Lisa turned the phone back around and tapped the screen again. "Last night I was thinking about it, and I started to put two and two together." She flipped the face of the phone back toward me. The cover photo was larger than it had been before. She pointed at the time and date in the bottom left corner.

By then I had reached the end of the printed pictures and had seen nothing out of the ordinary. I set the papers on the floor between us and leaned back against the porch railing. "I'm sorry, Lisa. I just don't get it."

Lisa picked up the papers. "Well, in the background...," she held the top photo up so that I could see, "in this corner there's a building. The Williston Hunt Club." She placed that picture down and showed me the next one. "This one, same thing. And again." She flipped through several of them and then stopped. "Now this is where it gets interesting. On this one, the building is demolished."

"Yeah," I said, trying to see where she was going with the whole thing. The building had been torn down during the timeframe that we were looking at.

"But, here's the kicker." She placed the photos flat into two stacks, one where the building was standing and the other where it was a pile of rubble. She turned both stacks around so that they were facing me. "Look at the dates." She pointed to the bottom right corner of one of the pictures and picked up her phone again. She pointed out the date on Cade's page.

"Yeah, so there's a big gap in time. So what?"

"A gap in time of like two weeks. I haven't mentioned this to you before, but something happened out there a few weeks ago. There were a lot of flashing blue lights. I could see them from my house. It was all kinds of ruckus, but nobody ever knew what it was."

So this event that she was talking about, whatever it was, happened during the gap in time. I finally began to see what she was suggesting—like everything else on the land, the incident would have been photographed with the camera. The pictures were missing.

"But they could have been deleted," I suggested and shrugged my shoulders.

"I thought about that, but look." Beside the time and dates was the name of the manufacturer of the camera. "They're different. It's two cameras. The Willistons are hiding something, Blake. What we are looking for is on that camera."

Now, I got it. "Dad won't be home for another five hours," I said.

"And Cade has FFA meetings on Wednesday afternoons. His parents are at work."

"We've got to go get it."

THE WILLISTON HOUSE stood in steadily increasing darkness. The place was surrounded by ancient oaks and towering magnolias that caused the late afternoon sun to cover the house in shadow. My stomach turned into knots. I was already in enough trouble, and if I got caught doing this...

I looked at my watch. We had exactly one hour before Cade's meeting would be over. It was four hours till Dad got home from work. We had plenty of time.

We were sitting in the cab of Lisa's truck. She had parked across the road from the house, deep in several acres of pine trees.

"I'm willing to bet that the camera is in the barn," she said.

I had been so focused on the house that I hadn't even seen the barn until she mentioned it. I looked to where Lisa was pointing. The old, ramshackle building separated the Williston's back yard from the field that was behind it.

I took a deep breath. "I'm ready when you are."

We left the truck hidden in the pines and ran across the road. With Lisa in the lead, we slipped around the side of the house and made our way across the back yard.

Finally, the barn loomed in front of us. Up close, the building looked ancient. It was a tall, lopsided structure that had each side stacked full of old lumber and tin. There were two doors. One door was at ground level and the other was higher up in the loft. The white paint on the bottom door was chipped and peeling. Three big letters had been cut from rusted tin and nailed above the entrance—WHC. It was the same letters that had been carved into the picnic table at school. At that moment, I realized with a jarring clarity what the trio of letters stood for—Williston Hunt Club. I felt ignorant that it hadn't occurred to me until now.

Lisa climbed the cinderblock steps. I was disgusted by the implications of what we were about to walk into. My stomach felt sick. Lisa flipped the latch, and the door swung open on its own.

I followed her inside. It was dark, but the wide gaps between the weathered boards let beams of sunlight through. Dust motes floated in front of us.

It was obvious right away that the barn wasn't used for farm related storage or use. A long piece of plywood rested on two sawhorses. The plywood was painted with two large triangles at each end. It was a makeshift beer pong table. An old, leather couch was pushed against the far wall. On the opposite end of the space was an old wardrobe and a short cabinet that held several drawers. Posters of half-naked girls were tacked to the walls. This was Cade's space.

Lisa and I were looking for the wrong thing. All we needed to pin on Cade was right in front of us. If we could prove that he and Tristan, collectively known as the WHC, had made a game out of hooking up with girls...

"I'll look in here. You get the cabinet," Lisa instructed and swung open the doors to the wardrobe.

I pulled open the top drawer of the cabinet. The metal wheels screeched against the old, rusty track. A sturdy, black cardboard box was inside. I removed the lid and could hardly believe what I was looking at. It was the camera.

"I've got it," I said. My heart was hammering in my chest as I picked up the camera and shoved it into the front pocket of my hoodie. After replacing the lid on the box, I slammed the drawer so forcefully that the whole cabinet shook. "Let's get out of here," I said.

We were almost to the door when we heard the unmistakable sound of truck tires on the other side of the wall. Lisa stopped walking and put her hand over her mouth. "Somebody's driving up."

From where we were standing, I could see through one of the large knot holes on the wall. I recognized the vintage truck. "It's Tristan." My heart skipped. "What is he doing here?"

"I don't know, but we've got to skedaddle." Lisa was looking around for somewhere to go. She grabbed my hand with hers. The skin contact sent sparks flying through my body.

A second later, I followed her up the stairs. The old, wooden steps creaked and shifted under our weight. We moved as quickly and quietly as we could.

The floor of the loft was scattered with loose hay. We stood still, careful not to make a sound. The gaps below our feet were wider than those on the bottom level. I could see Tristan enter the barn. He walked to the cabinet and pulled open the top drawer. I felt my jaw go slack. He opened the black box and reached his hand inside. He put something in his pocket and then shut the drawer.

Neither Lisa or I moved a muscle until we heard the sound of Tristan's truck starting up and driving away.

THE IMAGE OF Cade that I was looking at on the computer screen gave me goose bumps.

In the grainy, green-tinted night vision of the photo, Cade was kneeled down on the ground.

A large buck was laid across Cade's raised right knee. Each of Cade's hands grasped onto each side of the deer's antlers. The deer's tongue was lolled out in a disgusting and sad display of death.

An arrow was buried deep into the deer's side, and a dark trail of blood, black in the photo, ran from the entry point of the arrow all the way down the deer's side. Cade was smiling. Another boy that I recognized as being Tristan stood across from Cade. Tristan was holding a camera. He was taking a picture of Cade and the deer.

What we were looking at was from the hunting camera. The fact that it was the picture of someone taking a picture made the whole thing seem overly voyeuristic. I could see in the background, behind where Tristan stood, the rubble of the old building that was in the clearing.

Lisa and I were sitting at the desk in my room. She had removed the SD card from the camera and put it in the drive of my laptop. She had flipped through the pictures until she found the one that we were staring at.

"Like father like son," I said in reference to Cade's dad's prior record of being arrested.

"Yeah, but Cade wasn't *caught*. I think that's the thing..." Lisa was flipping through the photos on the computer and stopped abruptly. "O...M...G."

The picture that was now on the computer monitor explained it all...

Cade was standing next to Tristan. The deer was on the ground. A cop car was in the background.

Lisa flipped to the next photo.

A deputy was talking to Tristan and Cade.

"So they *were* caught," I said.

"But they weren't charged. Heck, nobody even knew about it, and around here that is an anomaly on its own." Lisa spun around so that she was looking at me. "I bet Cade's dad paid off this cop so he wouldn't talk. Just imagine the shit storm that would have happened if the mayor's son was charged with a crime."

"So what do we do now?"

Lisa shook her head. She clicked the X at the top right of the picture and closed the window. Cade, Tristan, the deputy, and the deer disappeared. "I'll figure something out. I promise." She removed the SD card from the computer. "Just imagine if this goes on social media... the scandal!" She waved the card in the air. "It could go viral."

I didn't like the idea of what she was suggesting. As much as I disliked Cade and what he had done, somehow this seemed wrong.

Lisa stood from her chair. She flung herself toward me and wrapped her arms around my neck. "We did it," she said. "Thank you."

I followed her downstairs, and, before she left, she turned around to face me again. "By the way, there's this thing Sunday night at the drive-in if you want to go. Since it's a full moon, they're showing a werewolf double feature. I thought of you as soon as I saw it."

Saturday would be the last day that I was grounded, and we didn't have school on Monday because of Labor Day. There was no reason that I *shouldn't* go.

"Sure," I said. "What time?"

"THERE'S SOMETHING WE need to talk about," Dad said.

We were sitting at opposite ends of the table. We were eating take-out. I was sure that he had found out about Lisa being at the house.

"I was offered a job," he said. "It's in Columbia. It's the same company I'm with now, but this will be better for both of us. We'll be leaving here in two weeks. I hate to do this to you now. I see you're making friends and all, but it's the choice I have to make."

I took a moment for everything to sink in. This was exactly why I hadn't wanted to make new friends. For months I had put a wall around myself to not let anybody get close, and, as soon as I let my guard down, something like this happens.

"What about Destiny? Is she moving with us?"

Dad shook his head. "We might be splitting up." I could see the disappointment in his eyes. "She thinks you don't like her anyway."

People with social anxiety often come across as standoffish, snobby, or uninterested. Since it isn't easy for us to interact with others, sometimes people think that we don't like them.

I left Dad by himself and went upstairs to my room. Since I knew I would be leaving in two weeks, was there really any point in continuing my relationship with Lisa? The truth of the matter was that I would probably never see her again. I knew that it would have probably been for the best to stop before I fell in love with her, but it was already too late.

But there was a way, I realized. In less than a year, she would be going to college. If I got accepted to the same school, we would only have to make it through eleven months of being apart.

CHAPTER THIRTEEN

THE NEXT DAY, Dad was at work, and I was home alone. The doorbell rang around lunchtime. The sound caused Wolf to go into a barking frenzy.

I stumbled through the house and made my way downstairs. Wolf had her front paws resting on the lower window panes of the door. Zee was trying to do the same thing but wasn't tall enough to reach. Each time that Zee tried to mimic the older and much larger dog, his paws just slid down the smooth wood. From the floor, Zee would start all over again. It was a display of sheer determination that I couldn't help but admire.

I peeked through the curtain on the door, but didn't see anything, mail carrier or otherwise. The day was bright and clear. Wolf's barking, however, was unrelenting. My eyes scanned the yard for a stray cat, squirrel, or anything that could have gotten the dogs so excited. Just as I was about to give up, I saw it... across the road, a dark figure moved among the trees.

It was a person wearing a long, black rain jacket with the hood pulled up. Now, he was staring straight ahead. Toward the house. At me?

With my hand, I felt the deadbolt to make sure that it was locked. I stepped away from the door and eased the curtain down, hoping that I had not been spotted.

Trying to be as quiet as possible, I moved into the living room and stepped closer to the bay window that faced the woods. From there I could get a better look. I pushed the edge of the curtain aside. The man was gone. My eyes darted to and fro in a frantic search. I would feel safer if I knew where he was. Then, from the left, he was on the porch.

I jerked my hand away from the curtain and stepped backward. My feet stumbled over the large rug that was spread across the floor. The corner of the coffee table caught my fall, but there was a loud clatter as everything on the table came down as my ass finally hit the hardwood. Now, it was impossible for him not to know I was in the house. From the floor, I watched as the dark shadow continued to move across the wraparound porch and stopped at the next window.

Wolf scampered across the room, barking at the figure that was on the other side of the glass. Zee was right behind her.

I got to my feet and ran. I didn't care anymore if I made noise. I bolted up the stairs, nearly tripping over my own feet before I reached the top. Once inside my room, I slammed the door and locked it. I ran to the desk, picked up my phone, and called the police.

BY THE TIME that the deputy got there, the man in the rain jacket was gone.

I was sitting at the kitchen table. The deputy was standing with his back against the counter. "So it was a man wearing a rain jacket?" Deputy Roper had a small notebook and pen. He was taking notes.

"Yes," I said. "I've already told you. Just like what I saw the other night in town at the gazebo."

Mr. Roper huffed, obviously annoyed. "Look, Blake. Unless you've been put in any physical danger, I can't do anything about somebody walking down a public road."

"He was on the porch," I explained. "He was wearing a rain jacket. It's not even raining."

"Blake, look. It's Spirit Week. I called the school. Today is Inclement Weather Day."

Of course. How could I have been so stupid? The fact of the matter was that there were probably countless people walking around the area wearing rain jackets and all kinds of other ridiculous things. The point of the day, after all, was to dress for extreme weather conditions.

The deputy continued. "Heck, I even saw a girl wearing a homemade costume that was supposed to look like one of those ice scrapers that you use on your windshield in the wintertime. She made it out of cardboard. Craziest damn thing I've ever seen. Have you ticked somebody off? Or upset somebody at school? I heard that you were suspended for fighting Cade Williston."

I nodded my head. I saw where he was headed with everything he was saying—it was Cade messing around with me, and by the time that Dad got there, the case had been settled, or at least as far as Deputy Roper was concerned.

"I'm going to head over to the Williston's," he told Dad. "I'll get a statement from Cade about where he has been all day." The deputy left.

"Blake, whatever is going on with you and Cade has got to stop," Dad talked in a low, hushed tone. "I can't keep doing this. It has been going on long enough. First, the night at the brewery, then the fight, and now this?"

I wasn't ready to tell Lisa about the fact that I would be moving soon, but I wanted to talk to somebody. Under the circumstances, the easiest person to talk to would be Charley17. There was no attachment between us. What was going on in my world had no bearings on his. And after all, the whole reason for him being in my life was to help me. When I logged on, he was already online. He messaged me right away.

How's it going?

NOT GOOD. I JUST FOUND OUT I'M MOVING TO COLUMBIA.

COLUMBIA. WOW. WE'LL BE SO CLOSE!

I wasn't expecting *that*. Before I could think of how to respond, I got a new message. This one was a photo. Until then, I hadn't even known that you could send photos on the site. It took a few seconds for the photo to load. Finally, the whole thing was revealed. It was an old, brick building. PALMETTO APARTMENTS, the sign said. The photo was accompanied by another message from Charley17...

WHAT DO THINK ABOUT THIS? WE CAN BE ROOMMATES. IT WOULD BE A BIG STEP UP FROM THE CRAZY HOUSE DON'T YOU THINK?

I flung myself back in the chair so forcefully that the wheels rolled across the floor. The chair didn't stop until I was a good three feet from the desk. I couldn't believe what I was seeing. My hunches had been right—the guy was a creep. Why did he think I would want to live with him? I didn't even know him. And how did he find out about my time at the mental hospital? All of that was supposed to be confidential.

During those two months I'd insisted that it was my fault that Davey was dead. I told the nurses that I would never let people get close to me again out of fear that they would get hurt. I had hoped that nobody would ever find out about all of that, but he did.

Trying to make sense of all of this, I had another thought—Charley17 was obsessed with me. I was sure of it. Internet stalkers were not that uncommon. Maybe he had been orchestrating things all along, trying to push the two of us closer together. The idea was scary. I knew I had to stop communicating with him before things got even weirder.

I went to the profile on my account and clicked a few links until I found the SETTINGS tab. I hovered the cursor over DELETE ACCOUNT for several seconds before finally clicking the button and sealing my fate. A message appeared on the screen.

THANK YOU FOR READING! YOU HAVE SUCCESSFULLY DELETED YOUR PROFILE. IF AT ANYTIME IN THE FUTURE YOU WANT TO SIGN UP AGAIN, JUST REACTIVATE YOUR ACCOUNT BY CLICKING HERE. GOOD BYE.

THAT NIGHT, I dreamed that I was a werewolf.

With clawed hands, I ripped at my clothes until they were in tatters. My rapidly growing muscles and changing bone structure pushed the pieces of fabric off my sturdy frame. Thick, brown fur covered every inch of my body.

I ran through the night and jumped from one bale of hay to the next. The feel of the cool air on my exposed anatomy was liberating. Eventually, I found myself standing outside of Lisa's bedroom window. The blinds were open, and I could see her lying in bed, asleep.

It was there, in the glass, that I saw my reflection for the first time. I had large, turned back ears and a long snout that was full of canine-like teeth. My back was slightly hunched, but the size of my pectoral muscles and biceps made up for the bad posture.

I tapped on the window, and Lisa woke. She shoved the blanket aside and stood from the bed. She was wearing a cotton tank top and sleep shorts. She opened the window, and I lifted her up. With Lisa in my arms, I ran.

I didn't put her down until I stopped at a small pond. Lisa sat on an overturned fishing boat, and I was on all fours lapping at the water. Lisa placed her fingertips on the flat of my stomach. The caress caused my body to flinch, and I stood up straight. Drops of pond water fell from my muzzle onto the top of her head. Finally, she slid her hand lower so that it was just below the slight paunch of my belly.

CHAPTER FOURTEEN

DAD WAS OFF on Friday, and he planned on spending the afternoon boxing up more things at the brewery.

I had an appointment with Mrs. Reynolds, so I rode with him into town. Dad parked in front of the brewery, and I walked over to the therapist's office.

At the beginning of the session, I told Mrs. Reynolds that Dad and I would soon be moving to Columbia for his job and that I didn't want to leave Lisa. I told her about the dream I had the night before of being a werewolf and how I carried Lisa in my arms. I felt myself turning red at the memory of the dream leading up to a happy ending.

"I think, subconsciously, you know that you are ready to change. Your true self, your essence, is wanting to break free. Accepting the past will allow you to move forward. Eventually you will have to face your fear head on."

I knew that she was right. All of this time I thought that if I let somebody get close I would risk reopening that wound. The only way that I could have a future with Lisa was to overcome the events of the night that Davey died.

Mrs. Reynolds stood from her desk and reached up to one of the highest shelves of the bookcase. When she turned around, she was holding an old, leather-bound book.

She returned to her seat and placed the book on the desk between us. "This is something that a colleague of mine wrote." She opened the cover and scanned through the Table of Contents. "Here we go." She flipped to the page that she was searching for. "Look at this." She spun the book around so that it was facing me.

What I saw on the page was a black and white sketch of a howling wolf. Below the image was an inscription—THE WOLF IS BELIEVED TO LEAD ONE TO JUSTICE.

"Trust your instincts, Blake. You're a smart young man. I think it would be a good idea to start trying psychodynamic therapy...," she began.

But I cut her off. "Pshychody-what?"

Mrs. Reynolds laughed. "Psychodynamic therapy. It's when you revisit a traumatic event and rearrange the effects that those things have on you. It teaches you how to deal with things in a different light. You can't change what happened, but you *can* take control of your future."

What she was saying caused me to remember something. One day, last fall, Davey and I had been hanging out in my room. Morris was home, but by that point he did very little with his days off. He never went out. He hadn't had a girlfriend that I knew of since Mom died in the car crash. I was no longer helping out at the pool store. Instead, I worked with Davey at Burger Heaven.

"It's bullshit, you know?" Davey spoke up.

"What is?" I was sitting on the floor, deep in the middle of a book. I looked up.

Davey was standing in front of me. He was holding the Groundhog Day box that Morris had helped me make ten years earlier. "This suggests that we don't control the things around us. I bet after you made it you just threw it outside and accepted the results as they were."

He was right. Back then, the entire second grade class had lined up the boxes along the sidewalk in front of the school. At exactly twelve o'clock we went to look. That day, the sun had been bright. There hadn't been a cloud in the sky. Every groundhog saw its shadow—predicting six more weeks of winter.

Davey removed the lid from the box and tossed it to the floor. He dropped the box onto the nightstand and lifted the table lamp. The lamp's cord pulled across the nightstand's surface and knocked loose change and a half empty cup of water to the floor. The cord remained plugged in, and it was pulled taught from the wall socket to Davey's hand.

"We're the groundhog," he said. "And this lamp is all the shit that goes on around us." He held the lamp over the box and moved it to the left and right, up and down. With his other hand, he shifted the box back and forth. "Watch the groundhog's shadow," he said.

I did. The shadow changed with each of Davey's movements.

"If we play things right, everything is in our control," he said.

Now, in Mrs. Reynolds office, my brain was being bombarded with so many different thoughts and suggestions. Some of them seemed to be at odds with one another, but really, all of it was true.

Some things we can control.

Others we can't.

The important thing is how we process and act on the things that happen to us.

After the session with Mrs. Reynolds was up, I went outside. The heat of the day was a welcomed change from the frigid temperature of her office. After I met up with Dad, I asked him if he had time for me to get a haircut. He said that he did, and we went across the street to Destiny's salon. While Dad waited in one of the barber chairs, Destiny cut my hair. It was the first time that my hair had been cut since the spring, and it felt good to have the shaggy mop off the top of my head.

Later, when Dad and I were walking to the car, I told him, "I just want you to know that I'm okay with Destiny going to Columbia with us."

"I'm glad I have your permission, but I wasn't going to let *her* get away. Even old men like me need some action every now and then."

"Ugh, Dad!"

He laughed and put me in a headlock. "I'm just messing with you," he said.

I elbowed him in the side.

I knew that the relationships I had with Dad, Destiny, and Lisa were headed in good directions, and I wanted to keep them that way. When I got home, I put the fifth sticker on my progress chart. This one was for maintenance.

CHAPTER FIFTEEN

LISA PICKED ME up on Sunday and drove me to her house.

"The 'rents are going to want to meet you before you're allowed in my room," she said. "Daddy's on the tractor, but Momma's out in the barn. Let's go."

The Tanners lived in a ranch-style house that had been constructed with red brick in the mid-seventies. The property was enclosed with a chain link fence.

Several buildings stood behind the home. One of them was a long shed that was open on both ends. It was where Lisa's dad kept his tractor.

"By the way, I like your new 'do." With her right hand, Lisa ran her fingers through my shorter hair.

We walked beyond the shed and past two smaller buildings that were made of plywood. The neatly mowed yard dipped and curved under our feet until we came to a building that was tucked so far back on the land that it had been out of sight until now.

"Here we are," Lisa said.

Personally, I would not have called this a barn. A barn was what was at the Williston's, but this...

The exterior of the building looked like something you could live in. It had tall, metal walls and carefully landscaped shrubs and flowers around the perimeter.

Once inside, I immediately realized that the building's primary purpose was to store the camper that was parked against the right wall. A large set of double doors hung at the opposite end of the building. It was where the camper could be driven in and out.

"Hey there," Lisa's mother spoke from across the width of the large space. She was on her knees with her hands deep in a five gallon bucket. When she stood up straight, I noticed she was wearing a pair of yellow rubber gloves that were covered in something dark and wet. She looked nothing like Lisa. She was tall and rail-thin. Her hair had been cut into a bob.

"Momma, this is Blake."

The older woman approached and held out her gloved hands toward me. I must have made a face because just a second later she pulled her arms back. "Oh, right, I would give you a hug, but, this..." She waved her right hand in the air and rolled her eyes.

"She's hulling black walnuts," Lisa explained. "They'll stain *anything* like crazy. Thus, the gloves."

"Oh," I answered.

"Lisa's told me so many great things about you," her mother said.

The idea that Lisa had been talking about me made me happy.

There was the sound of an approaching tractor. The throttle shifted down, and the tractor stopped. A minute later Lisa's father was walking through the door. Just like the last time I had seen him, he was wearing a flannel shirt and cap.

He held out his hand to me. "Jacob Tanner," he said. "It's good to finally meet you, Blake. I've been seeing you around. Lisa told me you're still trying to decide on where you want to go to school."

"Yes sir, I've been looking at a few."

"What do you think you might want to do for a living?"

Other than helping out at the pool store, the only job I'd had was the one at Burger Heaven in Ridge

Spring. "I'm not really sure," I told him. "I'll probably just go in undeclared and decide from there."

After a few more minutes of small talk, her parents went back to what they were doing, and Lisa and I went in the house.

Lisa's room was clean and girly. The bed was covered with a white comforter that had gray flowers printed all over it. A zigzagging line of lightning bugs was painted around the wall.

"They glow in the dark," Lisa said and flipped the light switch.

The room went dark, and each bug glowed a bright, fluorescent green. "It's glow-in-the-dark stars," she explained. "I stuck one on the butt of each and every bug."

Without turning on the light, Lisa moved to the desk that was pushed against the window on the opposite side of the room.

"Let me show you what I've come up with." She powered on her laptop. "Have a seat." She kneeled on the floor in front of the computer and patted the office chair next to her.

I sat down. I was expecting to see, at the very most, an edited and captioned photo of Cade that was ready to be posted on social media, but when Lisa opened the file, I was shocked at what was on the screen.

There was a photo of a road with a blank billboard, bright orange construction barrels, and a sign— Williston Plaza. Another picture was a close-up of the billboard. Next to all of this was a seemingly endless series of letters and numbers that I recognized as being HTML code that was often used for creating internet content.

"I figured out how to hack into the billboard at the Williston shopping center." Lisa tapped a few keys on the keyboard, and a new file opened up. It was the photo of Cade and Tristan from the hunting camera.

Lisa clicked on the image and dragged it to the billboard where it fit perfectly within the frame.

She enlarged the whole thing and let the cursor hover over the picture. An arrow appeared up on the right-hand side. She clicked it.

The photo of Cade and Tristan disappeared. In its place was another one from the same night—the one of the deputy talking to them. The deputy's body was circled in neon green. There was a caption—WAS THIS MAN PAID TO HIDE A CRIME?

Lisa clicked the arrow again. Now what I was looking at had a close-up of Cade on the left side and Mayor Williston's booking photo from when he had been arrested on the right. LIKE FATHER, LIKE SON, the caption read.

Lisa was smiling. "It'll go live on the night of the grand opening," she explained. "They're having a big party, and this is what they'll see."

For a moment I was speechless. What she was planning was way more than what I imagined.

"You're really good at this," I told her.

"Thanks." She continued to click around on the keyboard rearranging things just so. We were both quiet for a moment.

"Lisa, You know when your dad was asking me about college?

"Yeah."

"Well, I kind of lied. I *have* decided, but I wanted to tell you first."

Lisa stopped what she was doing and looked at me.

"I'm applying to Clemson," I said.

I was about to tell her the bad part—that Dad and I would be moving to Columbia, but before I had the chance, Lisa screamed, jumped up, and wrapped her arms around my neck.

When she let go and pulled back, our eyes met, and without hardly any contemplation, we were kissing. This went on for a few seconds, then her hand went underneath my shirt and mine went under hers. She sat up straight and slid to the floor.

"Your parents...," I said, trying to catch my breath.

By then she was unbuttoning my jeans. "This shouldn't take too long."

SHE WAS RIGHT. It didn't take long. At all.

Less than an hour later we were parked on the back row at the drive-in theater. What Lisa and I had done was just now beginning to sink in. Before that day, I had only kissed one girl—Katie Carmichael, who I worked with at Burger Heaven.

Kissing Katie had been a completely different experience. Davey had pushed me into it. "Just go for it," he'd urged me. One night, Katie and I had been sitting in the swing at my house, and I leaned over and kissed her. That was as far as it went, and it was the only time.

And now this had happened with Lisa. As daylight slipped into dusk, the full moon became visible. The way that the moon was positioned right above the movie screen couldn't have been more perfect. Both windows of Lisa's truck were down. There was a slight nip to the air. The breeze that came in carried the scents of popcorn, cotton candy, and fresh cut grass.

When the sky was finally dark, the first movie of the werewolf double-feature started. It was called *Cursed*, and even though the movie didn't scare either of us—we actually thought it was kind of funny, especially when the werewolf flipped off the main character. Lisa and I were huddled close together in the middle of the seat. We stayed that way, with my arm around her, all the way through the second feature, *Bad Moon*.

After the movies the field lights came on. I looked at the clock on the dash. It was already after midnight.

The cars and trucks were headed out of the parking area when, from my right, I heard a loud clatter. I looked and saw an old, green van making its way down the rough red-dirt drive toward the exit. At some point in time, the van's bumper had come loose and was now tied up with a bungee cord. The tie-job held everything in place, but it didn't stop the bumper from bouncing up and down and hitting the back end of the van as it moved.

The van came to a screeching stop behind us. The windows were so tinted that I couldn't tell who was inside. It looked like something that a serial killer would drive.

The passenger side window finally came down. A blonde girl I didn't recognize was in the seat. She was starring at me. I was confused. Then the driver leaned forward. It was Riley. "Blake," he called. "I didn't know you would be here." The person in the car behind him pressed down on the horn, telling Riley to go. "Why don't y'all meet us at Waffle House?" Riley suggested.

I looked at Lisa, who smiled, and I turned my attention back to Riley. The car behind him blared its horn again. "Yeah," I said. "We can do that."

The nearest Waffle House was fifteen minutes away in North Augusta at I-20. When we finally got there, the restaurant was full of people that must have had late-night munchies. There was no open booth; there wasn't even a spot at the counter.

"We can get take-out," Riley suggested. "We can go sit by the river."

While we waited on our food, the blonde girl, Lindsay, who was Riley's fiancé, was twirling her long hair around the fingers on her left hand. I noticed that her ring finger was bare and remembered that Riley had been saving his tips from the brewery so he could buy her an engagement ring.

"What did y'all think about those movies? Great or what?" Lindsay's eyes darted from me to Lisa.

After our order was ready, and we were back in the truck, Lisa and I followed Riley's van to the river. It was only a short drive down Georgia Avenue to where we eventually turned right, just before the bridge that would have taken us from one state to another if we'd kept going. We followed the looping road that eventually led us to the water.

We parked at a small gravel parking lot under the bridge. From there we followed a paved path that went downhill. The wide Savannah River was in front of us. The moon reflected against the water. Across the water the city lights of Augusta were bright. I thought about the story that Riley had told me about his girlfriend—while crossing the bridge to see him, she'd crashed her car and drowned in the river.

While the four of us sat on a pair of park benches and ate our food, the sound of the cars on the bridge above us was a nearly constant hum.

Later, Lindsay and Lisa were walking together along the edge of the water. Riley and I were sitting on the benches.

"It doesn't hurt to come back here?" I asked.

I could tell that it took him off guard for me to have realized that we were near the spot where it happened. "It took me a long time, but eventually I just said the heck with it, you know? Life's too short to be dwelling on the past. Instead of letting this be a place that made me feel sad, I focused on the happy times that I had here."

THE ROAD THROUGH the country was dark, but the high beams on Lisa's truck illuminated the landscape that lay ahead. By then the town and interstate lights were miles behind us.

On Sweet Water Road we were surrounded by cow farms, corn fields, and steep inclines of dense woods. There was only the occasional house to break up the rural landscape. On roads like this, deer were notorious for darting out of nowhere. That was my first thought when Lisa slammed on the brakes—she was trying to avoid a deer.

"Did you see that?" Lisa put the truck in reverse, backed up, and stopped.

A truck was several yards into the corn field on our left. Because of the flattened stalks in the truck's wake, it was obvious that the driver had lost control and run off the road. I recognized the decals on the back glass. It was Cade's truck. The headlights and brake lights were on.

Lisa pulled over to the side of the road. We left our doors standing open and followed the flattened path through the corn. The drying corn stalks clattered gently in the nighttime breeze. The red glow from the brake lights on the back of Cade's truck gave our surroundings the ambience of a Halloween haunted trail. I half-expected a masked man with a chainsaw to jump out any moment.

"I hope he's not in there getting frisky with somebody," Lisa said with a giggle that failed to cover up the nervousness in her voice.

Even at seventeen, I couldn't imagine being desperate enough for some action to go flying through a corn field just to find a private place.

By then we were right behind Cade's truck. Lisa walked around and stepped closer to the driver's side. "Cade?" Now, she was tapping on the glass. "Something's wrong," she said and was reaching for the door handle.

My thoughts about what could have happened to Cade were shooting in rapid fire...heart attack, stroke, blood sugar crash...I knew all of those things were rare in teenagers, but they did happen.

Lisa swung open the door, and the interior light came on. She screamed at whatever it was that she was seeing. I ran around the truck so that I was standing next to her, and I saw for myself...

The inside of the cab was covered in blood.

CHAPTER SIXTEEN

CADE WILLISTON HAD been struck over the head with an axe. That was the first thing that popped into my head.

At this thought, an unwanted memory flashed through my mind—my step-dad with a bloody axe, charging across the yard after me.

"Here, have another tea. It will make you feel better, I promise." Destiny sat a ceramic mug down in front of me.

Lisa and I were back home. After finding Cade's truck, we'd called the police, who, upon their arrival, got a statement from both of us and then abruptly sent us on our way so that they could investigate the scene.

I thought back to the idea that Charley17 had been orchestrating things to push me and him together. Obviously, he was a creep, but what if it was more than that? What if he was obsessed? What if he was the person wearing the rain jacket that had been following me around? When I deleted my Reading Buddy account, could it have caused him to finally snap? But why kill Cade? It just didn't make sense.

This was the second tea that Destiny had made for me. I lifted the hot mug to my lips and briefly inhaled the steam before taking a slow, careful sip. Destiny was right; the tea was soothing.

"Linden flower," Destiny said and poured herself a mug from the screaming kettle on the stovetop. "It helps to relieve stress."

It had surprised me to come home and find Destiny there. Maybe she and Dad hadn't broken up after all. The idea that Lisa and I might have interrupted something on the romantic side was kind of gross. That, in addition to the awkward run-in with Destiny the day before, made me feel weird being in the presence of the two of them together.

Lisa was sitting next to me at the kitchen table. Instead of tea, she had opted for hot chocolate. Dad stood across from us. He was leaning against the counter with his arms crossed. Destiny moved so that she was standing next to him.

"What were y'all doing out there?" Dad asked again.

"I already told you. We went to the drive-in." I knew that he wouldn't like that we'd gone to the river so I hadn't told him the rest.

"Okay, I got that part, Blake, but the drive-in's not on Sweet Water Road. There's no reason..."

"After the movie...," I relented, "we went to the river with Riley."

"Blake," Dad said. "You were at the river this late at night? You could have been robbed or even worse—you could have been killed."

"Well, we weren't," I shot back and immediately realized how inappropriate my words were, considering the apparent fate of Cade.

A knock on the door interrupted my thoughts. It was a police deputy. He was silhouetted by the flashing blue lights coming from the top of the car behind him.

Destiny sat her mug on the counter and opened the door. It was the same deputy that had been at the house a few days earlier. He looked at me as he made his way to the center of the room. Destiny returned to Dad's side. The kitchen door was left standing open, and the blue light that was coming through set me further on edge.

"We haven't found Cade, but we did talk to his BFF, Tristan."

I winced. Two dudes would *not* call each other BFF, but...whatever.

"He told us that it was possum blood in the truck," the deputy continued.

Lisa and I looked at each other confused about what the man was saying. I heard an audible sigh of relief from Destiny. Meanwhile, I couldn't shake the mental image of Cade killing a possum.

"Cade staged the scene to make it look like a murder. He was pulling a prank on you two." The deputy was looking at me and Lisa. "He wanted us to think that you killed him. Now, why would he want that?"

Why *would* he want that? Did Cade know that we found the images on the hunting camera? Maybe he had an idea of what Lisa was planning. It was obvious to everybody that we hadn't been getting along—maybe he'd seen this as the ultimate payback. But what about the fact that Tristan had also been at the Williston's barn that day? Like the rest of us, he was up to something. I couldn't let the deputy know all of that. Not now. Besides, it seemed like the sheriff, Deputy Roper's boss, was in on things, too. From what Lisa and I had been able to piece together, Mayor Williston had likely paid the sheriff to remain quiet, and that in itself was a crime. They would both be in trouble. If I brought up all of that, the shit would really hit the fan. I decided that once Cade reappeared, Lisa and I could settle this on our own without involving the adults.

I shrugged my shoulders at the deputy's question.

"The bad thing is," the deputy continued, "even though there is no sign of Cade being hurt, we still don't know where he is. We're waiting on toxicology results to determine that it is in fact possum blood in that truck. Meanwhile, I'm going to go over to the

Williston's place and see if I'm able to locate this boy. Then, maybe, we'll be able to get to the bottom of all of this."

CHAPTER SEVENTEEN

THE NEXT DAY, I was surprised when Dad made the suggestion that we spend the day at the lake.

I was sitting on top of the cooler that we'd brought, and Lisa was next to me in a beach chair. She was chewing on a string of old-fashioned licorice candy. In front of us, Dad and Destiny were chest deep in the black water. It was Labor Day, and the lake was packed with families and partiers who were wanting to hold on to the season for as long as they could.

But I was different—I was looking forward.

I was ready to move past all of this. Cade still hadn't turned up, and as much as I tried, I couldn't fully grasp the reasoning behind last night's prank. Tristan told the cops that Cade wanted to make it look like Lisa and I had killed him? But why?

The grand opening celebration for the shopping center was ten days away, and if Cade didn't reappear soon, the event would surely be canceled. Without the crowd, would it make sense for Lisa and I to go through with our plan for the billboard? And even if we did, would it have the same impact?

I still hadn't told Lisa that Dad and I would be moving away. The time just hadn't seemed right.

I looked out to the water. In the distance, a motor boat sped past and sent little waves across the water's surface. Dad and Destiny were laughing.

From out of nowhere, a group of screaming kids ran past. I could hear the squeak of the rubber floats that they wore, and, just like that, I was torn away from the book that I was reading and was back at the pool store in Ridge Spring. Davey was there with his nose deep in a book. In a split second, the image of Davey that I had in my mind was replaced with another one— here, he was screaming; blood was gushing from where the axe was buried deep in his ribcage.

Like the drama with Cade, it was time to put that to rest also. In less than a year's time I would be at Clemson with Lisa, and I didn't want to take any of that baggage with me. I thought about something that Mrs. Reynolds told me—"Don't let whatever lurks in the dark recesses of your mind control you. Face it, and conquer it." Just the night before, Riley told me that it wasn't until he finally went back to the river that he was able to overcome the loss of his girlfriend. As Mrs. Reynolds suggested at our last meeting, psychodynamic therapy is a way to rearrange a memory, and I knew that, in order to do that, I would have to go back to the house where the killing happened. There was one thing I wanted to take from there—a box that Mom had used to keep her favorite memories.

"I want you to go with me to Ridge Spring," I told Lisa and dug my toes into the sand. "I know, it sounds crazy, but..."

"It doesn't sound crazy." Lisa cut me off. "You need closure." She popped the last of the licorice into her mouth. "What time should this train depart?"

I DIDN'T WANT fifty questions from Dad about where I was going so we decided that we would wait until he went to bed.

At the intersection in front of the house, I was pacing back and forth, hoping that nobody would see me. My eyes kept watch on my surroundings. In the quiet night, every sound was intensified. Through the woods I could hear the distant clink of a dog pulling on its chain. Finally, I saw a pair of headlights approaching from the distance.

A minute later I was in the passenger seat of Lisa's truck, and we were flying down the road. There was hardly any traffic. Once we hit SC 23, it was a straight shot to Ridge Spring. We rode alongside the train track for miles through Johnston and Ward. Between the small towns, peach orchards and farmland stood on both sides. Some of the orchards had been re-planted the previous winter, and, in the moonlight, the white cardboard around the new tree trunks resembled rows of tombstones that would be found in a memorial cemetery.

"Are you sure you want to do this?" Lisa asked.

The town-limit sign was coming into view. WELCOME TO RIDGE SPRING.

"I'm positive."

The town looked the same as it had the last time I'd been there. Several grain silos greeted us right away. It was a single strip of stores that ran along the left-hand side of the street: a couple of restaurants, a bank, and an old-timey gas station, all of which were dark in the late-night hour. Except for us and a logging truck that barreled past, the road was empty.

The front of Heyward Pool and Supply was boarded over with plywood. The leader board out front said CLOSED. There was a For Sale sign in the window. The grassy area where the pool had fallen over and crushed Morris was roped off.

"Turn here," I said and pointed to my right.

Lisa turned the steering wheel and guided the truck onto a narrow, unlined road that was surrounded by wide hay fields and dark woods. "The driveway is up here on the left."

A rusty chain was blocking the path. The truck's headlights lit the long dirt drive that stretched and twisted its way through the trees on the other side. I got out of the truck, unclasped the chain, and let it fall to the ground.

After I was back in my seat, Lisa drove forward. The truck jostled back and forth when the tires hit the ruts in the packed red dirt. We went around a dense spot of oaks, and then the house came into view.

The yard was overgrown with tall grass and weeds. The months of abandonment and neglect had already taken their toll. The task of pressure washing the walls had been on Morris's to do list, but it never got accomplished. Now, the white asbestos shingles had a gray-green layer of mildew and grime. The rusted tin roof held a thick layer of leaves and pine straw. The front door was standing open, and the inside of the house was pitch black.

"This is kind of giving me the creeps," I said.

"Do you want me to turn around? Because...I can."

I shook my head. "Press on," I told her.

It had been three months since I'd been at the house, but a yellow police tape was still wrapped around the property. CRIME SCENE—DO NOT CROSS.

"Blake, I think we need to go. They obviously don't want us here..."

"Wait." I opened my door.

"What are you doing?"

"I won't be gone long." I grabbed the flashlight from the seat between us and jumped out of the truck. I ducked underneath the yellow tape and shined the flashlight around the property. I made my way up the concrete steps and was facing the open door. I hesitated and shined the flashlight in. The light was barely enough to cut a slim path through the darkness. Finally, I stepped inside.

The room that I was in held reminders of Davey's death. I tore my mind away from those things and back to the reason that I was there—Mom's memory box. It was in Morris's bedroom.

I continued through the den and noticed empty beer bottles scattered around the floor. Somebody had been coming into the house, probably local delinquents looking for a place to party.

The hallway was a long, cavernous space that had a series of doors on both sides—the kitchen, my room, a bathroom, and finally, at the end, Morris's bedroom.

I paused at the threshold of my old room and shined the flashlight in. Most of my things were gone. The bed was stripped. The last time that I had been there I was getting dressed to go to a party.

Eventually, I turned away and began walking further down the hall. The door to Morris's room was shut. I twisted the old doorknob and pushed the door inward. The inside of the room was a place that I had been only a few times, even when Mom had been alive, and even now, I felt like I was intruding on adult business. In the corner, Morris's work clothes were thrown over the back of the chair. The bed was made. I walked to the far end of the room and opened the closet. His clothes still hung in a neat row. What I was looking for was on the top shelf.

It was a slim, metal box that had a lock on the front. I slid the box off the shelf, tucked it under my arm, and was about to bolt from the room when the flashlight beam caught something else. Near the back wall of the closet, in the spot where the box had been, I saw a shimmer of purple. It was a fancy perfume bottle.

I picked up the bottle and pressed the spray pump. The scent was one that I recognized immediately. It was Summer Rose, the favorite of Davey's mother, Janice Steep. Smelling the flowery scent, I felt like she was there. What I was seeing added a new piece to the puzzle of that night.

I left the house with the memory box held tight under my arm and the perfume bottle in my hand.

CHAPTER EIGHTEEN

I CALLED MISS Steep as soon as I got home from school that Tuesday. She answered her phone after the first ring.

I could hear the TV in the background, and I imagined her standing in the living room with the cord from her old, rotary phone stretched through the doorway that led to the kitchen.

"I was just calling to see if you'd want to go to dinner. There's something I want to talk about."

"Blake, of course. I would love to see you. Is everything okay?"

"I'm fine," I told her. "See you tonight?"

It was dusk when she pulled up to the front of the house in her nice, jet-black sedan. Several bats were flittering around the sky over the driveway.

As soon as I opened the car's door, I could smell the perfume. The radio was turned to a jazzy classical station. Even after everything that had happened the past several months, Miss Steep had kept her movie-star looks and demeanor.

I got in the car, and she drove us to the diner on the square. With my suggestion, we sat in the back corner where there were no other customers in earshot.

The waitress brought us our drinks and said that she'd be back for our order. I could tell that Miss Steep was looking at my black eye.

"Do you still wonder *why* Morris did it?" I asked her after the waitress had wandered off.

Miss Steep looked up from where she had been contemplating what she would order from the menu. "All the time," she assured me. "But I don't think we'll ever know for sure."

From there, I cut right to the chase. "Why was your perfume at the house?"

Miss Steep's mouth dropped open and, for a moment, she was speechless. She looked confused. "Blake, I don't..."

Before she had a chance to finish, I reached into my pocket and pulled out a folded paper towel. With my hand hovering an inch or so above the tabletop, I flipped the paper towel open and let the perfume bottle roll onto the surface.

Miss Steep made a small but audible gasp of disbelief at what she was seeing. Her right hand shot to her mouth.

"It was in Morris's closet." I told her. "Next to some of Mom's stuff."

She carefully gathered her words before speaking. "Morris and I...we...I felt bad for him, Blake. He was all alone. I never told anyone about us because...," her eyes darted around the restaurant to make sure nobody was hearing, "after Davey died, I knew that, if people found out that your stepdad and I had been together, they would try to link what he did to that convoluted mess from mine and your momma's past. The last thing I wanted was for people to start digging all of that up. To me, that is water under the bridge. So... under the circumstances, I thought keeping the affair secret would be the best thing to do."

I was lost. This was the first time that I had ever heard the things that Miss Steep was bringing up. She knew Mom? And what exactly was this "convoluted mess" that she was talking about? "Under what circumstances?" I asked her.

Miss Steep lowered her hand from her mouth. Now, more than anything else, she looked surprised at the direction our conversation had turned. "You don't know, do you?"

I didn't answer her. Instead, I crossed my arms, flung myself back in the booth, and waited on an explanation.

"Blake, I thought you would have known by now." She leaned forward and propped her elbows on the edge of the table. Her voice lowered to a near whisper. "Your momma... you still don't know why she left your daddy the way she did?"

No. I didn't. All I knew was that, when I was five years old, Dad and Mom got divorced. There had never been an explanation given to me.

Like I've said before, I don't remember much about the days when the three of us had been a family. The things that I can recall are just brief images—a baby goat, a white picket fence, the vibrantly green tops of carrots in the ground, and a woman in a red cape tending a garden under the full moon.

After the divorce, Mom and I moved to Ridge Spring, and Dad went off to Georgia.

When I was seven, Mom remarried.

She died five years later.

"Your momma...," Miss Steep started again. "She took you and ran. It was to protect you," she said.

To protect me? Now I was prepared to hear the worst—I was ready to be told that Dad had done something horrible to her, or to me, or to the both of us, and I was now living with the bad guy. I swallowed the lump that had formed in my throat. "To protect me from what?" I braced myself for the answer. Was I ready for this?

"There were arranged marriages." The statement from Miss Steep was blunt. "Your parents were part of a community that set up marriages when the kids were very little, and your momma wanted to get you away from all of that. It was risky, but she did it to save you."

I must have looked at her with an expression that was one of all kinds of crazy because she returned my stare with one that was equally full of genuine sorrow. "Mom and Dad...," I said, "how long were they involved? Were they... part of those arrangements?"

Miss Steep nodded her head. "They're marriage was arranged, yes," she stated matter-of-factly.

Until then, I had believed that, despite their later differences in life, Mom and Dad had loved each other at some point in time when I had been a kid. But now Miss Steep was saying that they were forced to marry one another. Love had nothing to do with it. I shook my head. "No," I said. "You're wrong. They loved each other."

"The community had a person that they called The Sower. It was The Sower's responsibility to announce who would be paired together. On a full moon night, The Sower would plant carrot seeds in the garden. When the carrots sprouted, the green tops would spell out the names..."

As she was talking, I recalled something from the house where I'd lived with Mom and Dad. There had been a framed photo of a garden plot that hung on the wall in the hallway. In the picture, their names—James and Lisa—were spelled out in carrot tops that were shooting up from the dark soil. Was what Miss Steep telling me actually true?

The hazy image that I have from the full moon night, when I'd been peeking around the picket fence and watching the woman in the red cloak, now made sense to me. The woman was The Sower. She had been planting seeds.

All of this I was hearing was crazy. It was too much to take in. I stood from the booth. I had to get out of there.

"Blake, wait." Miss Steep reached up and touched her hand on mine. "Sit back down. There's a few more things that we need to talk about."

From where I was standing next to the table, I asked, "Like how you know about all of this?"

"I was part of it too, and I ran away not long after your mother."

With the knowledge that she had known my parents, even lived in the same community as them, my mind went back to that full moon night when I had been a kid watching The Sower in the garden from behind the picket fence. There had been someone else with me. It was a boy with hair so blonde it was nearly white. Davey. Until then, I'd thought that the day that Davey and his mother walked into the pool store had been the first time we'd ever met. Now, the realization that all of our pasts were tangled together was a punch to the gut. "I'm ready to go home," I said.

"Blake, we're not through talking yet."

"I said I want to go home. You can take me, or I can walk." I started to turn and make my way to the exit.

Relenting, Miss Steep reached to her purse. "I...just let me pay and we'll be out of here." She craned her neck to look around. "Waitress?" She waved the ticket in the air.

The waitress hustled over and took the ticket and debit card from Miss Steep. "We decided against dinner," she said. "He's... not feeling well."

"I'll be outside," I said and left Miss Steep alone in the restaurant.

The ride home was awkward, to say the least. We both sat in silence. Miss Steep had turned the radio all the way down to nothing. It was as if she was waiting on me, or her, to break the horrible silence that hung between us.

Finally, we pulled up to my house.

"WHY DIDN'T YOU tell me about Mom?"

Dad was sitting in his favorite recliner. In front of him, the TV was blaring some kind of obnoxiously loud action flick.

"What are you talking about?" He started to sit up, and I could tell that he had been sleeping.

"Mom, Dad. Miss Steep said that when y'all were younger you were both part of some kind of weird community that dictated who you would marry."

With the remote, he set the TV's volume to mute. "Why did she tell you that?"

"It doesn't matter *why*. What matters is that I get an explanation."

"Blake, I don't know how..."

"Tell me, Dad." My voice cracked.

He let the recliner's footrest down. It was a harsh, grating sound. He leaned forward, put his elbows on his knees, and buried his face in the palms of his hands. After a heavy sigh, he looked up at me again.

"Both of us grew up in that world. The community leader, The Caretaker, was the one that decided who we would marry. The Caretaker passed the names along to The Sower, and The Sower would..."

I nodded my head. I had heard all of this before, and I finished Dad's story for him. "She would plant carrot seeds, and when they sprouted it would spell the names of those who had been paired together. Miss Steep already told me, but what was the point of it?"

"It was supposed to be a self-sufficient community. We were living off the grid. We had our own law and order. We grew all of our own food. Everything was there for us. Even now, parts of it sound great, and I can see how somebody could fall for it. But the truth was that The Caretaker controlled *everything*. We gave our lives to him, and, in return, he decided how the course of our lives would go, who got what, and so forth. Your mom and I... we wanted to get out of it, and we decided that the best thing to do would be for her to split."

"So you never loved her?"

"Blake, it wasn't a matter of whether I loved her or not. The two of us getting married was what was going to be. We loved *you*, don't you see that? The only way for you to have a normal life was to get you away from it."

"Where was it? The community?"

"It was here," Dad said.

And my heart sank.

CHAPTER NINETEEN

THE NEXT DAY, after a night of fitful sleep, I got up early and walked through the hop yard alone.

The dirt road that cut through the acres of vines had become so dry that every step I took kicked up enough dust that it must have looked like I was leaving a thick trail of smoke behind.

After emerging from the field, I made my way to the spot where the original Williston Hunt Club once stood. I went to the center of the grassy area and sat down. I looked at my surroundings and imagined the old picket fence that used to run around the property. I closed my eyes, breathed in deep, and could have sworn that the musky scent of goat was drifting along the air.

How had I been so naïve that I hadn't realized I had been sent back to the place where I had come from? The same place that served such pleasant images from my past was also the place of lies and hidden things; things that only become clear by the light of the full moon.

With my right hand, I punched at the ground. I grasped the tall weeds in my fist and yanked. With my fingers bent into something that resembled claws, I dug down deep into the dirt.

From out of nowhere, a shadow spread over me. It was kind of like the effect of the sun disappearing behind a cloud, but this was different. I knew that somebody was standing there. When I looked up,

Tristan Clark was staring back at me. He was wearing a plain blue t-shirt and jeans. I realized that he must have been on the way to his morning classes at Tech. It was obvious that Tristan worked out. If he had come to the clearing for the purpose of kicking my scrawny ass he wouldn't have a problem. I must have jumped or flinched when I saw him because he laughed. "I didn't mean to scare you there, Blake."

"I wasn't expecting anybody to be out here," I told him as I took deep, lumbering breaths. My eyes darted to the opposite edge of the field where his old truck was parked. How had I not heard him drive up? I got up from where I had been sitting and stepped back, stumbling over my own two feet. "What are you doing out here anyway?" I realized that I had a clump of grass in my hand, and I tossed it to the ground. I hoped that Tristan didn't think I was throwing it at him.

"Looking for you," he said. "I just want you to know that I think what Cade did was stupid as shit," he told me. "You seem like a pretty nice guy, and I don't want to stand on the sidelines and do nothing." Tristan reached into his front jeans pocket. When his hand came out, he was holding his phone. He took a step toward me, and I stepped backward, away from him. "I'm not going to hurt you, bud," he assured me.

I stayed where I was, and Tristan continued to move forward until he was standing just inches away. He was so close that, when he talked, I could smell the spearmint chewing gum on his breath. "I want you to understand something. You don't need to be getting involved with Lisa Tanner," he said.

"Lisa's none of your business," I shot back. Besides, it was too late for not getting involved.

"She's not," Tristan agreed with what I said. "But she's also far from the perfect little angel you think she is." He held the phone so that both of us could see the screen, and I knew right away what I was looking at. It was a green-tinted image from a hunting camera, but I didn't recognize the location. With his fingers, Tristan zoomed in closer. A shirtless boy and girl were on the tailgate of a truck. The girl was straddling the boy's lap, facing him, and his right arm was wrapped around her back. His fingers were on the clasp of her bra. There were two things that I immediately recognized about the image—the girl's pigtails and the decals on the back of the truck. I was looking at Lisa and Cade.

I tore my eyes away from what I was seeing. I was disgusted. "That's...," I started, but couldn't think of the rest of what I wanted to say.

"I'm just doing this for your own good," Tristan said.

I realized then why he'd been at the Williston's barn the day that Lisa and I had seen him there. There must have been other hunting cameras in the cabinet, and he'd been getting the SD card from one of them. He must have gone home and loaded the files onto his computer and then used his phone to take a picture of the monitor so he could bring it with him that morning. In some kind of twisted way, he thought that, by showing me, he was helping me out.

Finally, I gathered up the rest of my words and continued. "Cade must have manipulated her into it. I know all about the WHC, and how y'all..."

"You're right," he cut me off. "The things Cade and I did were wrong, but I'm not hear to talk about that stupid club. I'm done with all of that." Tristan closed the image and put the phone back in his pocket.

"What are you here to talk about then?"

"Lisa," He stated bluntly. "Listen, he was only with her one time, and afterwards she wouldn't leave him alone about it. She latches onto you, Blake. She won't let go."

I shook my head. "You're crazy," I told him.

"There's something about her. It's like she gets obsessed with you or something."

"That doesn't make sense," I told him. "If that was the case..."

"Once she realized that Cade didn't want to have anything else to do with her, she was determined to keep their little fling secret. She doesn't want anybody to know how much of a skank she really is."

"You're no different." I realized that I had started to think of Cade and Tristan as a single unit—The WHC. I wanted to punch him. I wanted to hit him harder than I had hit Cade that day at school. I wanted to knock his teeth out and make his nose bleed. I wanted Tristan to walk away from the fight with *two* black eyes compared to my one.

I threw the weight of my body onto him, and both of us fell to the ground. I was on top of him, and I raised my fist high over my head and brought it down onto his chest. When I tried to hit his face, Tristan blocked my blows with his arms.

His hands eventually grasped onto my forearms. He was a lot stronger than me and was able to hold me off. Eventually, he put all of his strength into what he was doing and flipped me over. The back of my head thudded on the ground so hard that I actually saw a brief flash of white.

I think I went out for a second, but, when everything settled again, Tristan was straddling me. I tried swinging my closed fists at him, but all I was able to do was brush his shirt.

Finally, he let me go and hoisted himself off me. He sat down next to where I was lying and started brushing the grass and dirt off his jeans. "Believe me, you don't want to do this." He chuckled. And he was right—I didn't want to fight him. That had been a really bad idea. I rolled over and pushed myself to my feet. By then, Tristan was standing. "There's one more thing I wanted to show you." He reached into his back pocket. He pulled out a folded piece of paper and tossed it toward me. "I don't understand it. Cade found it in his dad's stuff. Just think about the facts, okay?" And he walked away.

I unfolded the piece of paper and couldn't believe what I was looking at. It was a picture of carrots growing in a garden. The green tops spelled out two names—Davey and Lisa.

When I got home, I slammed the door so forcefully that the framed pictures rattled on the wall. Dad had already left for work, and I went upstairs to shower and change clothes.

Under the hot spray of water, I did what Tristan suggested—I thought about the facts, and there was one thing that bothered me more than anything else. Lisa had been lying to me all along.

THINGS AT SCHOOL went downhill. My mind was so preoccupied with everything else that was going on that I could barely pay attention in any of my classes.

If I had thought that everybody had been avoiding me before, now it was like I had the plague. I got death-stares from most of the students for just walking down the hall. I realized what Cade's prank had done. It had turned all attention toward me—the worst thing you could do to somebody with social anxiety.

It got so bad that I even avoided the picnic table on my lunch break. I figured it was possible that Cade could turn up any minute, and if he did, he would be out there waiting around the corner of the building just like he used to. So instead of going outside, I sat at a corner table in the cafeteria by myself.

The day trudged on like this, and I thought the final bell would never get there. Mrs. Reynolds had been right. Cade's latest prank was a crafty one. In the classes that he and I shared, I looked at his empty desk

from where I sat in the corner and thought to myself—
he has the upper hand, and he's not even here.

I WAS ON the school bus when I heard that Cade was
dead.

It was raining, and the bus was moving extra slow
through the downpour. It seemed like it would take
forever for us to reach the drop-off spot in front of my
house, and I just wanted to escape.

The news had spread through the bus the way I
imagined a virus would work its way across the
programs on a computer, crippling each one in its path.
Nobody approached me and told me personally, but I
heard it from the guy sitting in front of me who was
whispering the news to his friend.

Soon, everybody had their phones out, texting and
reading the story on social media. A girl who was
sitting several rows up from me burst into tears
because of what she was learning. I wondered if she
had been another one of Cade's conquests.

Just to make sure that what I was hearing wasn't
another of Cade's pranks, I pulled my own phone out of
my jeans pocket. After connecting to the internet and
searching for CADE WILLISTON, the first thing that came
up was an article from a local TV station. It had to be
true if it was on the news, right? I clicked the link and
began to read.

According to the reporter, around two-thirty that
afternoon, Cade's body was found in the woods about a
mile from where his truck had been abandoned in the
corn field. It appeared that he had been attacked with a
sharp object.

I turned off my phone, closed my eyes, and took a
deep breath. My stomach clenched itself into a tight
ball. I felt sick. It was no secret that Cade and I hadn't
been getting along, and I knew what all of this must
look like.

I thought about what Tristan told the cops two nights earlier—Cade had smeared the inside of his truck with possum blood because he wanted people to think, even for the briefest of moments, that he had been murdered. After setting the prank, Cade hadn't made it far.

The bus finally stopped in front of my house, and I stood from where I was sitting on the back row. I didn't look at anybody as I walked down the aisle, but I could feel their eyes on me.

I pushed my umbrella open as soon as I was off the bus, and I started walking toward the house. Just a few seconds later, I heard the revving of the bus's engine behind me. I stopped and looked over my shoulder.

From the other side of the bus windows, the other students were staring at me. I knew what they were thinking—I killed Cade.

Lisa was already at the house when I got there. She was sitting on the top step of the porch. The overhang of the tin roof shielded her from the falling rain. When she saw me approaching, she stood. I could tell by the look on her face that she already knew what happened.

"We have to get rid of all of it," I told her. "The pictures, the hunting camera, all of the stuff you made for the billboard, everything. If the cops find out how far all of this has gone... if they see how much we hated Cade, you know what they'll think."

Lisa shook her head. "They'll find out anyway, Blake. And if we hide everything, when they *do* find it, things will only be a thousand times worse."

"Well then," I said. "We tell them the truth about everything."

"That's what I'm saying."

"No. I mean we tell them *everything*. I know about you and Cade. I saw pictures, Lisa. Why have you been lying to me?"

"What are you talking about?"

"Tristan showed me pictures of you and Cade." I grabbed her arm. My grip was too tight. It was probably hard enough to leave a bruise. I hadn't meant to be so forceful.

"You're hurting me," she said.

I loosened my hold, and she jerked her arm away. She knew she had been busted. She started down the steps, but she was stopped dead in her tracks by the deputy's car that was pulling in the driveway.

WE TOLD THE deputy about Cade and Lisa, the probability that Mayor Williston had paid off the sheriff to remain silent on his son's night-hunting offense, the WHC, our plan for sabotaging the grand opening of the shopping center, and that we'd seen Tristan sneaking around the Williston's barn the same day that we had been there.

But, even after all that, I suspected Charley17 may be the one to blame for Cade's death.

"So let me get this straight," the deputy said. "You think that this Charley person you met online is obsessed with you. He started sending you weird messages over the internet, you think he has been following you around wearing a rain jacket, and now, because you deleted your account, you think he might've snapped and committed murder?"

I nodded my head.

"Hell, at this point, I'm not ruling out anything. Can you show me the profile?"

"I'll get my computer," Dad said, and he left the room. He came back a minute later with his shiny silver laptop in both hands. He placed the computer in front of me on the table and pressed the power button.

The deputy moved around the table so that he was watching over my shoulder. I clicked on the browser search bar. After going to The Reading Buddy site, I found Charley17's profile, but when I clicked I got the message that the it had been set to private.

"It looks like I'll have to re-open my account and send him a new buddy request." I clicked on the LOG IN tab and was able to reopen my account by entering my password. Then I clicked back to Charley17's profile and sent him a buddy request. "Now we wait for him to take the bait."

It was just a minute later that the computer dinged with an incoming message. The quick response time caused my skin to crawl. Charley17 had already accepted my request.

YOU AND CHARLEY17 ARE NOW BUDDIES. START READING AND SHARING.

"That *is* creepy," the deputy admitted. "Go to his profile before he realizes that something might be up. Do it before he has a chance to think that he is in some kind of trap."

I clicked on Charley17's profile picture, the werewolf mask. "See, it's empty," I told him.

"Send your login info to this email." From over my left shoulder, the deputy slapped a ripped corner from his yellow paper onto the table. "Pronto. We'll get a cyber team that will be able to trace everything to see where Charley's messages are coming from. Hopefully we'll get this case solved before ya'll move to Columbia."

Lisa looked at me, and her mouth dropped open. I, like her, was speechless. Her finding out like this was the last thing that I wanted. She jumped up from her chair and stormed off. I followed after her, but she was already out the front door, and by the time that I was on the porch, she was halfway across the driveway.

"Lisa!" I yelled after her.

She spun around so that she was facing me. "How long have you known, Blake?"

"A few days," I admitted. "I was going to tell you that day we were at your house, but..."

"But we started fooling around," she said. "I see how it is. They drew you into their little games, didn't they?"

"What are you talking about?"

"Cade and Tristan. You're just like them. You're only after one thing."

"No. It's nothing like that."

"I'm going home," she said.

CHAPTER TWENTY

JUST WHEN I thought that things couldn't get any worse, they did.

The day after Cade's body was found, Mrs. Reynolds decided that it would be best for me to withdraw from school. The plan was for me to resume my education once I got to Columbia. Dad's job allowed him to take the rest of the month off so that he could prepare for the move.

With both of us being at home, the process of packing up the house was kicked into high gear. By the time that mid-afternoon rolled around, most of the living room and dining room was finished. I was pulling the roll of tape across the top of a box when the doorbell rang. Dad was already on his feet, and he went to the door.

From where I was sitting on the floor in the other room, I could hear the voices. Dad was talking to Deputy Roper. "Is Blake around?" The deputy wanted to know.

"Yes," Dad answered, "Is something wrong?"

"Well, Mr. Thomas, there's something I need to talk to both of you about."

Then there was the sound of the door shutting, followed by heavy steps across the floor. "Blake," Dad called. "Deputy Roper's here. He needs to see you."

By then I was already standing, and I went into the foyer where I leaned against the doorframe with my arms crossed.

Deputy Roper looked at me and nodded his head before he started speaking. "We found Charley," he said. My heart skipped at the mention of my Reading Buddy, who I suspected of stalking me and killing Cade. "But here's the thing," the deputy continued. "There is no way Charley had anything to do with what happened to Cade Williston." Out of the corner of my eye I could see Dad glance in my direction. "You *were* right about one thing though. Charley *is* in Columbia, but here's the kicker—he's been in a mental hospital the whole time. They've had him on suicide watch for the past eight months. It's impossible that he would be anywhere but there."

On the day that Charley had sent me the creepy message about wanting to live together, he'd said that he thought that the apartment he picked out would be a big step up from the crazy house. Now I knew that he hadn't been talking about *my* time in the mental hospital. He had been referring to his own.

"The guy has a long history of being abused by both of his guardians," Mr. Roper continued. "It really messed him up. His therapist thought it would be a good idea for him to join The Reading Buddy site. He thought it would be a good way for Charley to begin to interact with others."

That made sense. After all, it was that line of reasoning that Mrs. Reynolds had pushed me to do the same thing.

Dad spoke up. "So what do we do now?"

"Well, we have to look at all of this from a different angle. The fact is that Cade Williston was murdered, and somebody, most likely a local, knows the answer." Deputy Roper was still looking at me, and I tore my eyes away from his stare. "If either of you think of anything else, don't hesitate to give me a call." The deputy went to the door, opened it, and looked over his shoulder before stepping outside. "I have a feeling that all of us will be talking again real soon." And then he left.

As soon as the door was shut, I let myself slide down the wall so that I was sitting on the floor. Both Wolf and Zee came over and crawled onto my lap. They were pawing at my arms and licking my face. Dad looked at me and said, "We'll get through this. One way or another, everything will be okay."

Eventually, I got to my feet and went upstairs to my room where I let myself fall backward onto the bed. I stared at the ceiling and let everything begin to sink in. All of us—me, Lisa, Davey, and Cade—had been linked together our entire lives. A long time ago, Lisa and Davey were assigned to be together. Lisa had lied about messing around with Cade. Now, Davey and Cade were dead. All rationality pointed to either me or Lisa killing Cade, and I knew I didn't do it.

Until then, the darkest moment of my life had been when I'd been trapped underneath the overturned pool with my dying stepdad. Now I felt like I had lost everything. Lisa, college, all of the progress that I had made—none of that mattered any more. I was done. I got up and yanked the progress chart off the wall, wadded it into a tight ball, and threw it across the room.

I went back to the bed where I eventually fell asleep and dreamed that I was dead. I was in a closed casket and could hear the dirt being thrown on top of me. Eventually, my eyes shot open, and I knew that I wasn't ready to be buried underneath all of this. I reached into my shirt and wrapped my hand around the pendant that Riley had given me. The oak tree was a symbol of strength. It was time to set things right. I clawed at the lid of the casket until it splintered into pieces, and I dug my way through the soft dirt, finally emerging zombie-like under the glowing moon.

When I woke it was dusk, and I was filled with hope. Back on the night that my stepdad had been running behind me with an axe, I had been sure that the keys in my hand would be my salvation.

I stood from the bed and went to the closet. The door was standing open, and I reached inside to the top shelf where there was an old, raggedy shoe box that I picked up. With the box in my hand, I lifted the top and dropped it to the floor. I reached inside and dug around the loose change and trinkets until I found what I was looking for—Morris's key ring.

There were at least a couple dozen keys on the thing. In addition to the ones for things around the household, there were also the keys for the pool store. I searched through them all until I found what I was looking for. It was a small skeleton key with a round end. On the opposite side of the room, Mom's memory box was sitting on top of the desk. That was where I went next.

With the metal box in my lap, I sat on the floor and leaned my back against the bed. Mom always said that only happy memories were allowed inside. *Defining moments*, she called them. After she died, I would often look through the contents to remind myself that those things had in fact happened. For the first time in nearly a year, I put the key into the latch. The hinges squeaked when I opened the lid.

Inside were snapshots of Mom and Dad, her and Morris, and several of me at various ages. One picture in particular caught my attention—I must have been four or five. I was standing in front of a shabby picket fence where I was feeding a carrot to a little black and white goat. Amid all of this, there was something that I had not seen inside the box before, and the sight of it now broke my heart—it was the paper groundhog that Morris had drawn for me. I picked it up and traced my thumb over its surface.

After Davey was killed, people often asked how it was possible that someone could go from making paper groundhogs to committing murder. They, like me, wanted to know *why* he would have done it. Even though there seemed to be no motive, there was proof. There was video footage taken from the nearby bank's ATM camera of him running across the road with the axe in his hands. They found a loaded pistol next to his body under the pool.

I felt tears pooling in my eyes. It was a punch to the gut to realize that Morris had been sentimental enough to add the paper groundhog to the box of Mom's most cherished memories. I placed the cutout back on top of everything else and took a look at the pile. Despite all the lies and secrets that had shaped most of my life, everything inside that box represented a simple truth.

And at that moment in time, the truth was exactly what I needed.

The wadded progress chart was next to me on the floor. I picked it up and tried to flatten it out, but it was a crumpled mess. Regardless, I peeled the last sticker off its backing and stuck it to the final step—TERMINATION.

CHAPTER TWENTY ONE

I TOLD MRS. Reynolds everything I knew about the community where I had come from.

"Those kinds of situations can lead to all sorts of psychological problems," she said. "With that kind of upbringing, all kinds of things can happen. People are more likely to develop obsessive disorders or become risk takers. Low self esteem, anxiety, dependency, and delinquency are all common."

Afterwards, while I waited on Dad to pick me up, I went across the road to the library that stood on the opposite corner.

The interior of the old building was quiet. From what I could tell, there were only two other patrons there. An old man was sitting in one of the big, comfy chairs by the door reading the newspaper, and a woman was looking through the rows of audio books.

I went to the center of the floor near the circulation desk where there were several public computers with the library's catalogue. I found the call number range for books that dealt with mental issues and, with a ball point pen that someone had left behind, I wrote the numbers on the palm of my hand.

I walked up and down the rows and followed the call numbers until I eventually found the area that I was looking for. I scanned over the book spines and let the titles speak for themselves. Eventually, I found two books that I slid off the shelf, and then I walked to the end of the row.

Under the current circumstances, I didn't want the books on my checkout record, nor did I want the keyword searches on my own computer. So I was left with only one option. When I was sure that no one was looking, I lifted my shirt and slipped both of the books into the waistband of my jeans.

Before stepping through the door, I reminded myself that I wasn't stealing the books—I was borrowing them, and I planned to bring them back. I didn't slow down as I exited the building. One time Davey told me, "If you ever shoplift, never *ever* pause at the door. It only shows that you are nervous about something."

I STAYED UP late that night reading the books and thought about what Tristan said about Lisa—"She latches onto you and won't let go." Well, maybe he was right. Maybe she *had* become obsessed with me. That, I could kind of agree with, but was it possible that she could be a killer?

The fact of the matter was that I could relate parts of what I was reading to all of us—me, Lisa, Cade, and Davey. Maybe all of us had been effected by the same thing—the place we came from. And there were a few more answers I needed about that part of my life.

When I thought that Dad was probably asleep, I stepped into the hallway and was careful to not make too much noise. I was in my socks and holding my boots in my left hand. I glanced toward Dad's room. The door was shut, and I could hear him snoring. It didn't take long for me to realize that Wolf had followed me. The sound of her claws on the hardwood gave away any amount of secrecy that she could have hoped for. She stopped and looked at me with a pair of confused, sleepy eyes. A second later, Zee also stepped out of the darkness of my bedroom. The puppy yawned and took his spot behind the older dog.

I tiptoed closer to them and held my finger upright in front of my lips. "Shhhh," I whispered. Wolf must have understood what I was saying because she titled her head to the side and perked her ears. She turned around, nudged Zee with her nose, and both of them went back to their beds on the floor.

Once I was downstairs, I reached into the back pocket of my jeans and pulled out a small square of paper. On it was a note that I had written for Dad. I stuck the paper to the mirror of the hall tree.

IF YOU WAKE UP BEFORE I'M HOME, PLEASE DON'T CALL THE POLICE. I'M OK. LOVE YOU!

Then I reached to the little peg board that hung on the wall next to the door. There was only one set of keys—Dad's. I had contemplated taking my own truck, but by that point in time it had been underneath the tarp and not driven for months. What if the battery was dead? The sound of the engine trying to turn over would have been too much. I gently wrapped my hand around Dad's set of keys and clutched them so tight that I could feel the pointed ends and jagged teeth pressing into the skin of my palm. I eased the keychain off the hook.

Once the keys were free, I breathed a sigh of relief and steadied myself for the next step. I was almost there. I turned the door's latch as quietly as I could, and once the door was open, I slipped outside, closed the door, and locked it.

Standing on the porch steps, I put my boots on and then ran across the yard. After I was inside the cab of Dad's truck, I pulled the door close to the side of the truck body, but I didn't shut it all the way out of fear that it would make too much noise.

I fumbled through the keys on the ring until I found the right one. I put the key into the ignition and turned. The diesel truck roared to life. It was too loud. I looked toward Dad's bedroom window and was relieved to see that the light hadn't come on.

Holding the door with my left hand, I backed out of the driveway, and once I came to a stop at the intersection, I pushed the door far enough so that I could give it a good pull. Once the door was shut, I put on my seatbelt.

Then, I drove.

THERE IS A place just outside of Trenton where the road twists around a sharp curve that sits high above everything else. To the left is a steep drop-off to a woodsy stretch of land that has a train track running through the bottom. The road is so high that the top of an old, abandoned building is almost level to the guard rail.

Davey and I used to sit on that roof for hours at a time, reading and smoking cigarettes. One time, Miss Steep smelled the smoke on us and confronted me about it. "Davey doesn't. It's only me," I told her, lying and taking the blow for my friend. "I knew Davey wouldn't," she said. "And I don't want you to either. It's a nasty habit."

I drove around the curve and down the steep hill that led to a small neighborhood of recently constructed townhomes. I pulled up to the front of the house that I was looking for. Miss Steep's convertible was parked out front. The car, in addition to the light that was shining through the house's left side window, was a sure indication that she was home.

I knocked on the door and looked at my watch. It was close to ten o'clock. I hoped that it wasn't too late to be there. I knocked a second time and still got no answer. Finally, just as I was about to give up, I heard the click of the deadbolt from the other side, and the door eased open.

From inside the house, Miss Steep peeked through the narrow crack that was between the door and its frame. When I glanced down, I saw that her hand was still on the doorknob. She was ready to push the door closed if she needed to. She looked over my shoulder toward Dad's truck. "You drove?"

I nodded my head. "Can we talk for a minute?" I asked her.

I could see the contemplation and hesitation in her eyes. "Is it okay if we meet somewhere? My house is a total mess. If I would have known that I'd be having company..."

"Sure," I told her.

"What about Scramblers out on Highway 25?" She suggested. "They're always super busy."

SCRAMBLERS WAS LOCATED in the annex of an old gas station. To say that the restaurant was busy was a vast understatement. The place was hopping.

As soon as I opened the door to the twenty-four hour diner, I was blasted with the sounds of old country music, clinking dishes, laughter, and chatter coming from every direction. I hadn't been hungry before I left home, but the smell of frying bacon and eggs caused my stomach to rumble.

I looked around the cramped interior and saw that Miss Steep had already arrived. Thankfully, she was able to get a corner booth where we would be out of earshot from most everybody else that was there.

I made my way through the crowded restaurant and took my seat in the booth across from her. After we ordered our drinks, I began talking. "In these arranged marriages that you were telling me about, what if something happens and the two kids, when they turn eighteen, are not able to marry?"

I looked around, reached into my pocket, and pulled out a piece of paper that I immediately unfolded and laid on the table between us. It was the printout that Tristan had given me. Her son's name and that of the girl that he was intended to marry stared back at her. Davey and Lisa.

"Where did you get this?"

"Let's just say somebody gave it to me, and we'll leave it at that." I didn't want to get into anymore detail about Cade and Tristan than I had to. "What do you know about Lisa?"

"I never really knew her, Blake. They adopted her when she was a baby."

"Adopted?" That single word added a new twist to everything that I was learning.

Miss Steep nodded her head. "I always thought that the man, Lisa's adoptive father, was kind of whack-a-doo, if you want to know the truth."

"Whack-a-doo how?"

"Years ago, after your momma ran away, things within the community started to crumble. It didn't take long for the whole thing to come crashing down. After your dad moved away, that seemed like the end of it. I stuck around for a few more years. It was just me, the Willistons, and a few others, but eventually it collapsed. Mr. Williston was The Caretaker, and he still blames your parents for the beginning of the end. Without the community under his control, he had no interest to stay part of it. Without a Caretaker, it seemed done for. Then that girl's family showed up. He was determined to get the whole thing back on its feet. He said that he was going to be the new Caretaker. By then Mr. Williston was on to bigger things, he wanted to be mayor, and he passed the reigns of Caretaker over to Mr. Tanner. Davey and Lisa were both toddlers at the time, but they were quickly assigned to one another."

Even after I'd started to accept all of this, the way she said that they were *assigned* to one another still gave me the heebie-jeebies. "So they got somebody new to be The Sower?"

Miss Steep looked confused. "I was The Sower all along."

I had always thought that the woman in the picture of me feeding the carrot to the baby goat had been Mom, but it wasn't. It was her, Miss Steep.

I was letting this knowledge sink in while Miss Steep continued. "But, like your momma, I took Davey and ran."

"So, what is the possibility that Lisa would have been assigned to someone else after Davey was gone?"

Miss Steep shook her head. "None. The moment of assignation is as good as marriage. The community looks down on divorce. Even if a spouse dies, we were forbidden to start a new relationship. Why are you asking me about all of this? Do you think it has something to do with Davey and Cade Williston dying?"

"I... to be honest with you, I don't know *what* to think anymore."

"Lisa hurt you didn't she?" The change in conversation was abrupt. "I can see it in your eyes when you talk about her. You love her, and she hurt you." Miss Steep reached out her hands and placed one on each side of my face. Her hands were cold. "Look me in the eyes, Blake Thomas, and you tell me the truth."

The truth. It was what everything seemed to be coming down to. My thoughts were interrupted by the flashing blue lights of a police car that was pulling into the parking lot. My heart began to thud.

"I couldn't save Davey," Miss Steep continued, and I could tell that she was rushing her words so that she could get them in. "I'm afraid the same thing that happened to Cade might happen to you." She dropped her hands from my face.

By then, Deputy Roper was standing next to our booth. He was looking at me. "Your father called and said that he woke up and you weren't at home. The truck was missing."

Dad walked up and was standing behind the deputy.

"I left a note," I started to explain, looking past Mr. Roper at Dad, and I realized how ridiculous the statement really was.

"Blake, now is not the time," Dad cut in. "Let's go home."

I stood from the booth and walked out of the restaurant with Dad and Deputy Roper, leaving Miss Steep behind.

Once I got to the parking lot, I realized that Dad had ridden there in the police car, and now he was going to drive both of us home in his truck. As he steered the truck onto the road, I glanced through the restaurant's window at Miss Steep one more time. Even from the distance, I could tell that she was shaken by everything that was happening.

CHAPTER TWENTY TWO

SOMETHING WOKE ME up. It was a soft thud against the window pane. I was getting out of bed to investigate, and I heard it again. I looked at the clock. It was just after midnight. Once I was on my feet, I walked across the room and stood in front of the window. What I saw through the glass sent chills down my spine.

Lisa stood at the edge of the hop yard. At first glance, I thought she was wearing a white dress, but it was actually a t-shirt that was several sizes too big. The moon made the fabric seem to glow. She had on a pair of denim shorts that were barely visible.

With her right hand, she threw something toward me. Whatever it was thudded and bounced off the glass. It took me a second to realize that she had a handful of scuppernongs. She was throwing them one by one trying to get my attention. She must have finally noticed that I was up because she dropped the grapes to the ground, reached into her back pocket, and pulled out her phone. A second later, my phone, which was across the room on top of the dresser, dinged with an incoming message. I went to look.

WILL YOU COME OUT HERE SO WE CAN TALK?

I went back to the spot in front of the window. Lisa was staring up at me. It was obvious that she was waiting on a reply. I still hadn't made up my mind on the way I felt about her or what she was capable of, and just when I was about to type LEAVE ME ALONE, I saw movement in the rows behind her.

Someone stepped out of the field. It was the man with the black rain jacket, but now there was something different about his appearance.

Lisa must have heard the movement because she turned to look. When she saw what was standing behind her, she turned to her left and bolted into that side of the field. The predator ran after her. My mind had been going down the wrong path. Lisa had nothing to do with Cade's murder, and now she was in danger.

I was acting on impulse when I spun on my feet and ran across the room. I realized that I could call the cops, but I knew that by the time that they got there Lisa could be dead. I had to go help. In my determination to get out of the house, I must have made a lot of racket and scared Wolf because the dog jumped up from the bed, barking her head off. Zee followed suit. I tripped over the door jamb and slammed into the hallway wall. Dad's bedroom door jerked open. "What's going on?"

I didn't slow down. "Call the police." I yelled back at him. "Now." I rushed down the steps and through the front door.

I RAN THROUGH the hop yard as fast as I could. Twigs and rocks jabbed at my bare feet. Because of her white shirt, it was easy to spot Lisa running away from me in the distance. I watched her go into the old tractor shed that stood outside of Mr. Callaway's vineyard. A blur of black plastic went in after her. I was gaining ground on both of them, and, in no time, I was in the building too.

The floor had never been poured with concrete, and the dirt below my feet was so dry that it felt like I was running through powder. Old tires and rusty farm tools were everywhere. The inside of the building stunk like something had died. An antique tractor was dead-center of the space, probably in the same spot where it had been parked and left decades earlier. The front-end of the tractor was facing me, and the enormous back tire stuck out so far to the side that I had to turn sideways to maneuver past. I made it, and from where I was, I saw Lisa and her pursuer exit the far end of the building.

I had to duck underneath the upright harvesting equipment that was on the back of the tractor. Once I was on the other side of the machinery, I stood up straight and took a few more strides before I ran face first into a furry, cold, stiff *something*. The nastiness of whatever it was caused me to instinctively jerk away. I stepped back to get a good look.

It was a possum. No, *three* possums. The dead animals had been hung from the rafters so that their pink noses were facing toward the floor. Even in the darkness of the shed, I could see that they had been cut open. The source of the reeking odor was now evident.

Cade must have killed the possums out there and never made it back to dispose of the carcasses. That had been three days earlier, and the heat of the Southern September had caused the dead animals to have a stench that was agonizingly brutal. Being so close almost made me gag. I held my breath and pressed on.

The man in the rain jacket appeared in the doorway. It was obvious that he had come back for me, and I wondered—had I been lured into a trap? Planning my escape, I knew that there was no way that I would be able to make it back to the other side of the farm equipment fast enough.

My eyes scanned the shed, and I noticed a tall stack of wooden crates on my right. I moved slowly toward the exit. The man stepped closer to me, and when I thought that the time was just right, I reached out my hand and shoved the towering stack of crates toward him. The whole thing toppled over, but the impact didn't knock him off his feet. Instead, the fallen crates created an obstacle that he would have to get past. Hopefully it would buy me enough time to make it out alive.

I made it to the back end of the shed and, as soon as I ran through, I realized what stood in front of me—Mr. Callaway's vineyard.

I REMEMBERED HOW I once thought that it seemed possible to get lost in the scuppernong field at night. Maybe I could lose my pursuer in the thick of it. I ran as fast as I could to get there.

I ducked underneath the first row and then the second. I went on like this until I was deep in the field. Then, only after I felt like I was a good distance from the maniac, I ran straight down one of the rows.

I heard Dad calling my name from somewhere in the field. He was out there looking for me. A second later, I realized that he wasn't alone. Blue lights were flashing in the distance.

I stopped where I was and crouched down low so that my head couldn't be spotted bobbing along the trellises. If I stay here, I thought, either the police or Dad will find me before the killer does.

From my right, a gloved hand shot through the vines and grabbed onto my shoulder. I jerked away from the grasp, spun around, and scooted myself backward just as the maniac pushed through the vines. I scrambled to my feet and ran in the direction of the police car. At the end of the row, my feet slipped, and, to steady myself, I wrapped my hand around a small tree that was growing there. The slickness underneath my feet, in addition to the grip that I had on the tree, caused me to spin around.

I fell backward into a mushy, sticky pile of goo. My hands came up and were covered in slimy gunk.

Whatever it was that I had fallen into smelled ripe like fermenting wine. That was when I realized that it was the spot where Mr. Callaway threw baskets of overripe scuppernongs that were no longer suitable for selling.

When I looked up, the man was standing over me. The rain jacket's hood had slipped off his head. It was Jacob Tanner, The Caretaker and Lisa's adoptive father. I looked past him and realized that Deputy Roper had found us. He was running in our direction. He was holding a flashlight, and the beam danced across the ground in front of him as he moved. "Hands up," Mr. Roper yelled, and Mr. Tanner did as he was told. Behind the deputy, Dad emerged from around the corner. He had his arm wrapped around Lisa. Somehow, she had escaped. Dad and Lisa ran to where I was standing. I stepped out of the slop I was in and let both of them wrap their arms around me.

I watched Deputy Roper handcuff Mr. Tanner. Some of the words Miss Steep said to me earlier that night replayed in my mind—"I'm worried the same thing that happened to Cade might happen to you."

THE REASON BEHIND Jacob Tanner's actions was easy to explain—he had been protecting the creed of the community. People wanted that easy, straightforward kind of answer for Morris killing Davey, but there wasn't one.

The reality was that a series of secrets and lies had led us to where we were. Some psychiatrists say that people with social anxiety are wearing a mask. They say that there is a fear of honoring part of yourself. And, for me, it was true. The reality of Davey's death was something I knew I would have to face sooner or later, and I was at the point where I was ready. It was time to let Morris rest in peace. Finally, if somebody were to ask me what I was hiding, I would tell them the truth— my stepdad didn't kill Davey Steep. I did.

CHAPTER TWENTY THREE

THE DAY BEFORE we moved to Columbia, I asked Dad to drive me to Ridge Spring one more time.

Even though I hadn't talked to Katie Carmichael since the day before Davey died, I still had her number in my contacts. She was who I needed to see. She was a key player in the events that led to Davey's death, but I didn't know the complexity of it all. When she answered the phone, I noticed right away that her voice sounded timid. Eventually, she agreed that we could meet.

At eleven o'clock that morning Dad dropped me off at Burger Heaven, where Katie still worked. It was too early for lunch and too late for breakfast. There were only two other cars in the parking lot, both of which belonged to employees.

Shallow rain puddles stood all along the black asphalt. Because of the front that had brought the showers, the weather had turned considerably cooler. I zipped my jacket and shoved my hands deep into the wool lined front pockets.

The building that stood in front of me was gray and dingy looking, but the logo on the sign was simple and bright—the name of the restaurant was spelled out in blue and had been crowned with a yellow halo. A pair of white angel wings stuck out from the B on BURGER. People say that once you get to heaven you will be at peace with everything. I didn't know what I thought the real heaven would be like, but I hoped that it was nothing like this.

I saw Katie's car making its way down the road. It was the same car that she had saved her money to buy. She was proud of that car. The right turn signal came on, and she pulled into the parking lot. I noticed that the rear-end was dented, and I wondered if she had been in an accident. I hoped she was okay.

She got out of the car and locked the door. She shoved her hands deep into the pockets of her hoodie and went to the front of the building. Except for a quick glance in my direction, she did nothing else to acknowledge my presence.

I followed her inside. The doors of Burger Heaven have always cracked me up. A set of decals with the image of a gate printed on each one was stuck to the glass. It was supposed to be that, when you walked in, it was like you were walking through the gates of heaven itself.

The inside of the restaurant smelled like grease. At first glance I only saw one person working. It was a girl that I didn't recognize. She was wiping down the counter. Then I noticed Tommy, the twenty-something guy who was the manager. He had his back turned and was busy filling a to-go order. I followed Katie to a corner booth.

Then...

FRY DUTY WAS the worst assignment you could have at Burger Heaven, but I loved it when Katie was there.

Katie was a year older than me and had just gotten a promotion to shift supervisor. She was beautiful. She was a little shorter than me and had brown hair that she liked to pull back in a loose ponytail. Somehow, she even made the little white visors we had to wear look cute.

The position of the frying station was perfect for checking out Katie's rear-end whenever she would bend over to get a tray from one of the low shelves.

After closing that night, we walked to our cars together. I had parked next to her. It had been two months since I'd kissed her, and there seemed to be no awkwardness between us. Both of us acted like it never happened. After she unlocked her door, she looked at me. "What are you doing tomorrow night? I'm going to a party if you want to go with me."

"Yeah," I told her. "I'd like that."

Now...
"HOW HAVE YOU been?" I asked her. "How's work?"

Katie ignored the small talk and cut right to the chase. "Why did you want me to come here, Blake?"

"You called me, remember? And I never called you back..." It was true. On the night that Davey died, I had received a phone call from her.

"That was three months ago," she said.

"My phone..." I started to explain how it had been yanked from my hand and crushed on the concrete, but she cut me off.

"I needed your help."

Then – 9:25 pm...
I OPENED THE front door and was about to put on my boots when Davey's black Transam skidded over the gravel in the driveway. He stopped so that his car was between the house and my truck.

As soon as Davey got out of the car, I noticed he was wearing his Burger Heaven uniform—a blue shirt and khaki pants. The restaurant closed at nine o'clock, and Davey usually went home to change clothes before he went anywhere else.

"Where are you off too?" He was walking toward me.

"I'm going to a party with Katie," I told him.

"I thought you were done chasing after her." Now, Davey was standing on the bottom step below me. Bugs swarmed around the porch light over my shoulder. "We're friends aren't we, Blake?" The question took me by surprise.

"Of course," I told him. "What are you talking about?"

He shook his head. "You can't be friends with me *and* her," he said.

My phone rang, and I looked at the screen. "That's her now. I'll ask if its okay for you to tag along."

Before I had a chance to answer the call, Davey jerked the phone from my hand, threw it onto the concrete steps, and crushed it with the heel of his boot.

"Man, what the hell?" I bent over to pick up my phone and noticed Davey was walking away.

I thought he was going to his car but he went around the side of the house. When he came back he was holding the axe from the wood pile. "Best friends are supposed to stand together," he said.

Now...

"DAVEY WAS STEALING small bills from the register," Katie began. "It was never a large amount—just a buck or two here and there. He must've thought that I was in the restroom, but I'd only stepped around the corner. When I came back I saw the whole thing. The rest of the night was busy, and when it finally started to slow down, Davey shut down the fryer. I confronted him and said that I would have to report it to Tommy. Davey had the fry basket in his hand, and he looked like he was about to fling the hot oil on me."

The fact of Davey stealing money wasn't new to me. I'd known it, but I never said anything. Several times I'd even been with him when he shoplifted at the mall. I was never brave or dumb enough to do it myself, but I'd known. I wondered if not telling made me just as bad as him.

"That's not all," she continued. "I sent him home early, and I had to close the store by myself. When I got to my car it wouldn't start. I was trying to call you to come pick me up."

Now, everything was starting to make sense. With mine and Katie's stories merging together, all of the pieces were beginning to click into place.

Then – 9:29pm...
WE WERE BACK inside, and Davey tossed the axe onto the couch where it landed with a soft thud on top of the thick, leather cushions.

For a moment, I thought he was ready to talk things out, but then he walked across the room to the gun cabinet. He jerked the drawer open and grabbed Morris's pistol and a box of bullets.

"Davey, what are you doing?"

"I'm going over there myself." He started walking toward the door.

"What's going on?"

He stopped and turned around so that he was facing me. "What makes you think something's going on?" He opened the box, reached inside, grabbed a few bullets, and dropped the rest to the floor.

"I don't know. I'm just trying to understand..."

"Understand what?" A string of spittle flung from Davey's mouth and landed on his chin. The pistol was loaded, and he closed the chamber. He raised the gun and pointed it at me. "What do you know?"

I grabbed the axe and stood up straight. The next two things happened all at once—the gun fired, and I swung the axe.

Now...

KATIE UNCROSSED HER arms, put her hands together, and placed her elbows on the table. "I kept calling, but you never answered so I called my sister to come pick me up. I figured you had stood me up. The next day we had the car towed to the shop, and the mechanic told us that there was sugar in the gas tank. That was why the car wouldn't start. As soon as he said it I suspected Davey."

In Davey's mind, Katie had become an enemy, and I was stuck in the middle. If I went, I would be taking her side over his.

Then – 9:32pm...

BLOOD WAS GUSHING out of Davey's side. He raised both of his hands to cover the wound, but the blood sprayed through the gaps between his fingers. This seemed to go on for an eternity, and he finally fell face forward onto the carpet.

I dropped to my knees and crawled toward him. I tried to pull him into my arms, but his bulk was too much for me to lift. I hadn't meant to kill him. I'd only wanted to stop him. When I let him go, my shirt was drenched. I crawled away and huddled in the corner between the couch. I wasn't trying to hide anything, but I had to get the bloody clothes off. I couldn't stand the stickiness any longer. I stood up and stripped down to my boxers. I left the pile of clothes on the floor and went to my room where I put on a pair of flannel pajama pants.

When Morris got home I was sitting on the couch. I wasn't wearing a shirt. The loaded pistol was in my hand. Morris had been across town trying to finish cutting an old lady's grass before it got too dark.

"Blake," Morris ran over and kneeled next to me on the floor. "Blake, what happened?"

"I didn't mean to." I told him.

Morris picked up the axe from where I'd dropped it to the floor. I'm still not sure what he was going to do with it, but he looked at it as if he was trying to figure things out.

That was when the reality of everything snapped into place. I had to get out of there. I jumped to my feet, shoved the pistol in the pocket of my pants, and grabbed the keys from the table by the door.

Morris was right behind me. He probably didn't even realize that he was still holding the axe. He was yelling for me to stop. I made it to my truck and was about to unlock the door when I realized that the keys I had in my hand were not mine—they were Morris's.

I ran toward the Pool Supply store and locked myself inside. I think I understand now that Morris was afraid. When he shattered the glass, he was trying to get to me before I hurt myself.

Now...
"WHY DIDN'T YOU tell somebody?"

Katie shook her head and shrugged her shoulders. "It wouldn't have mattered. By then he was dead. I never told anybody about the money either. Everybody thought that Davey was perfect. He was the smart, good looking kid that everybody wanted to be friends with. I imagined that people would have thought that I was making it all up so I decided it would be easier to just let it all die with him."

Then –10:03PM-daybreak...
AFTER MORRIS BUSTED his way into the store, I jumped up from where I was in the stockroom, left the pistol on the floor and slammed through the back door. Morris wasn't too far behind. "Blake, wait. Let's talk about this." He caught up with me, reached out to grab my shoulder, and I tripped. The weight of my body falling against the pool brought the whole thing down.

With my stepdad's crushed, lifeless body lying close to me, I had more than enough time to dwell on everything that had happened. In the darkness, my mind rambled. There was no way people would believe I had acted in self defense, I thought. I'd been dumb. I'd run away from Morris when he was trying to help.

Not long after Mom died, Morris told me something—"You're all I've got now," he'd said. "You are the only person I have in the entire world."

On the other hand, if Miss Steep found out the truth about her son, it would destroy her.

I came up with a plan. There was nobody that the lie would harm in the same way that the truth would have hurt Miss Steep.

I thought I had the perfect way out.

Now...

AFTER OUR MEETING, Katie and I walked to the parking lot together.

"Let's keep in touch," I told her before she got in her car. After she drove off, I called Dad to come pick me up.

One day, down the road, all of this would be a memory. But I also knew that the truth of Davey Steep's death would undeniably shape the rest of our lives, for better or worse. I had no idea what would happen once I admitted everything.

Mrs. Reynolds had often told me that one day I would have to face my greatest fear, and my greatest fear was this—the truth. I was afraid of the consequences and the inevitable change that would come with it. It was obvious that the events of the past had effected all of us, but the truth would likely take things into another direction.

"Turn in here," I told Dad, pointing to the driveway on my right.

"What? The police station?"

"There's something I need to tell them."

ONE YEAR LATER...

I WISH I could say that I had overcome social anxiety, but it's not that easy. The most important thing was that I was getting better.

"I'm headed out to my interview," I said and peeked into the kitchen where Destiny was busy preparing dinner. Dad was at work and should be home soon.

Destiny looked up from where she was chopping vegetables on a cutting board. "You look great," she said. "I hope you nail it."

I was wearing a button down shirt that was tucked in and everything. My hair was neatly trimmed. And my face had even started clearing up.

Zee, who had grown a lot over the year, stood on his back legs and reached his paws toward me. I took one in each hand, leaned down close, and let him lick me on the face. The old lady that Zee was named after said her name meant "God's helper", and she must have been right because the dog was like a guardian angel to us. I don't know how we would have gotten through Wolf's passing without him.

The weather was cool, and it was starting to drizzle rain. After I got in my truck, I drove to the end of the driveway where I stopped to get the mail from the box. There was a letter that was addressed to JAMES THOMAS AND FAMILY. I was family, so I ripped it open. It was an invitation to Riley and Lindsay's wedding.

There were two signs on the doors for the newest location of Burger Heaven—OPENING SOON and NOW HIRING SHIFT SUPERVISORS AND CASHIERS APPLY WITHIN.

Once I entered the restaurant, I spotted Katie right away. She was now going to college in Columbia and had gotten the Assistant Manager job at the new restaurant. She was busy stocking supplies and teaching a new cashier how to run the register, but she took a minute to look up at me and smiled.

I was a few minutes early so I took a seat in one of the booths while I waited. I was busy reading a book on a new app that I had downloaded to my phone when something on the other side of the glass caught my attention—there was someone wearing a black rain jacket with the hood pulled up that stepped into the restaurant. She pushed the hood back. It was Lisa. She spotted me right away and walked over to the table. She was smiling.

"What are you doing here?" I asked her.

"Applying for a job," she said. "I'm going to USC."

I was saved from the uncomfortable situation by a man wearing a tie. He had a clipboard in his hand, and he was walking toward the table. I knew he must be the manager. "Well, look, I've got an interview. I'll see you later, okay?"

"I can't wait."

MY EYES SHOT open. I had been dreaming.

At first I thought I was home, but the hard, uncomfortable mattress reminded me that I was in the hospital, and it was not the *get well soon* kind. This was the crazy house. Once the realization dawned on me, I wished that I was back in that dream world where everything seemed to have worked out for the best. Instead, I was reaping the consequences of what I had done.

From the other side of the door, there was the sound of a key and then that of the lock turning. The door opened, and the nurse entered. "It's time to go," she said.

I stood from the bed.

"Here's your name badge." She was holding a rectangular sticker and a pen.

I took the pen, wrote my name in the blank space, and slapped the sticker to the front of my shirt. The nurse escorted me out of the room.

The quarterly social was held in the central hallway. They had set up a folding table with chips, cookies, and some type of orange punch. One of the nurses had connected her phone to a little speaker and was playing music.

I avoided everybody, the patients *and* nurses, and went straight to the snacks. I was ladling punch into a plastic cup when somebody said my name from the other side of the table.

At first the voice set me on edge, but then I remembered I was wearing the name badge. I looked up to see who had spoken to me. The other guy was about my age and had short, black hair. He was wearing a t-shirt that had the screen-printed image of a vintage werewolf mask on the front.

It can't be, I thought. There is no friggin way.

My eyes shot to the name badge on his chest, and I dropped my cup of punch.

HELLO. MY NAME IS CHARLEY.

THE END

ABOUT THE AUTHOR

BRYCE GIBSON writes fiction that takes readers to charming and oftentimes sinister areas of The South. He lives in South Carolina with his wife and their dog.

To learn more, visit him online at
BRYCEGIBSONWRITER.COM

CPSIA information can be obtained
at www.ICGtesting.com
Printed in the USA
BVOW03s2248201117
500961BV00001B/40/P